CW01261753

SURVIVAL

REVENGE OF THE LIVING DEAD

SHAUN HARBINGER

THE UNDEAD RAIN SERIES

Rain
Storm
Lightning
Wildfire
Survival

1

It was late morning, with the sun beating through the *Big Easy*'s portholes, when I rolled out of bed feeling like I'd just gone ten rounds with Mike Tyson.

The cabin was bright and hot and smelled distinctly of sweat. I needed to get out of here and get some fresh air before the contents of my stomach—burgers and pasta mixed with a liberal amount of red wine and beer—came spewing out over the bed.

Groaning as a bolt of pain speared my head, I opened the door and stumbled up the stairs to the living area. It was no less bright or warm in here and the smell of greasy burgers and alcohol hung in the air. I pulled open the door to the aft deck and threw myself outside just in time to throw up over the side of the boat.

A couple of minutes later, as I spat the last remnants of acidic bile and bits of burger into the sea, I heard a chuckle floating over the waves. I looked up to see the *Lucky Escape* anchored off our port side and Sam standing on her foredeck. He wore red swimming trunks and a white shirt printed with large red palm trees. He also wore a shit-eating grin on his face.

"Dude, I told you to slow down last night," he called. "You were chugging that wine like there was no tomorrow."

"Well, unfortunately, there *is* a tomorrow," I said, "and it has arrived."

He chuckled again. "Alex, you need to take it easy, man. We're going ashore later and you need to be on top form."

"Top form isn't achievable today," I told him.

"Well then, you'll be zombie chow."

"Thanks for that, Sam."

"Just telling it like it is, man." He turned away from the railing and went below deck.

I sank down onto the bench that curved around the bow of the boat and willed my head to stop hurting. It didn't work. Why had I drunk so much last night?

Deep down, I knew the answer. Since seeing my father and brother at Camp Achilles a month ago, I'd been in a funk that had been difficult to shake. I wasn't moping around like a moody teenager or anything like that but every now and then, I'd feel so down that I wouldn't know what to do. Everything seemed hopeless.

Last night, the four of us—Lucy, Tanya, Sam, and myself—had eaten together on the *Big Easy* and we'd all partaken of a case of wine we'd looted from a shop last week. After the wine had gone to my head, I'd foolishly decided that a few beers would be a good idea and had drunk at least four bottles of ale we'd taken from the same shop as the wine.

I'd been trying to forget, to banish the black dog of depression that had been hanging over for me ever since I'd seen Joe and my dad.

My plan had worked for a couple of hours and I'd spent the evening in a fuzzy cloud of merriment.

But it had only been temporary and now I was paying for it.

Getting gingerly up from the bench, I took a deep breath of salty air and walked through the living area before pushing through the door that led outside to the sun deck. As I'd expected, Lucy was there, lying beneath the beating sun in her yellow bikini with a pair of shades over her eyes. She was lying on a dark blue beach towel that she'd spread over the deck and her long blonde shone in the sun like a golden halo.

She was a work of art and I couldn't help but

appreciate her even in my less-than-optimal state.

"Hey, Alex," she said, surprising me. I'd thought she might be asleep but her eyes were obviously open behind the sunglasses. "How's your head?"

"It's been better," I told her. "I shouldn't have had so much wine. Everything is bright and I feel hot."

"Take your T-shirt off, then. It's way too warm to be wearing that thing."

I looked down at the 'Sail to Your Destiny' T-shirt I was wearing, aware for the first time that I'd gone to bed fully-dressed. As well as the T-shirt, I was also wearing my jeans. No wonder I was melting.

I took my jeans and socks off but left the T-shirt on. Even though I'd lost a lot of weight lately, I still felt self-conscious every now and then, even around Lucy. Feeling cooler in my boxers, I sat, cross-legged, on the deck next to her. The day was cloudless, the sea calm, and in the distance, I could see the south-east coast of England. A slight breeze cooled the sweat on my face and bare legs.

"Do you want to talk about it?" Lucy asked.

"Talk about what?"

"Last night. The last couple of weeks. How you're feeling?"

I shrugged. "I just keep thinking about my dad and my brother stuck in that camp, believing that the army is going to keep them safe. We've seen what happens to the camps once the zombies decide to attack."

"You asked them to come with us and they refused. There's nothing else you could have done, Alex." She sat up and put a hand on my shoulder. "I know this has been bothering you ever since you saw your family but you have to stop beating yourself up about it."

"You're right," I said. "But It'll probably just take some time."

"Of course it will," she said softly, squeezing my shoulder. "Now, why don't you put some music on and we can chill for awhile before we go ashore?"

That sounded like a good idea. I needed some time to recover from last night's excess before I tackled a food run. I went into the living area and turned the radio on, wincing as Def Leppard blared out of the speakers. Why was everything so loud? Grabbing a pair of sunglasses from the counter, I put them on and retreated to the aft deck, then climbed the ladder up to the bridge where the pulse of the music was still audible but wasn't so deafening.

Sitting on the pilot's chair, I leaned my elbows on the instrument panel and put my head in my hands, silently pleading with my headache to go away.

I'd only been there for what seemed like ten minutes before the radio crackled and a voice came through the static.

"This is Echo Six. Does anyone copy? Over."

I sat up in the seat but didn't key the radio. This sounded like a military unit calling others in the area. Our past experience with the military had been both good and bad, but the bad had taught me it was best to stay out of their way. So I thought it best not to give away the fact that we were close enough to receive this broadcast from Echo Six.

After a couple of moments, the voice spoke again. *"This is Echo Six. Does anyone copy? Over."*

I glanced at the clock on the wall and realised that what I thought had been a ten-minute nap had actually lasted an hour and a half. The headache was becoming duller but now my neck and shoulders felt stiff from sleeping in such an awkward position.

"This is Echo Six. We require immediate assistance. Is there anybody out there? Over."

Echo Six wasn't getting any response to his call for help. His voice, which had seemed calm when he'd begun broadcasting, now held a note of urgency. *"Is there anybody out there? Anyone at all?"* I heard another voice, someone in the same room as the speaker, say, *"It's no good, Sarge. No one can hear you. We might as well accept that we're not getting out of this."*

"This is Echo Six," the original speaker said into the radio. *"Mayday. Mayday. Mayday."*

I don't know what it was about that broadcast—maybe the note of panic in the speaker's voice, maybe the fact that the other person there seemed resigned to his fate—but something made me pick up my own radio and press the Talk button. "Echo Six, I hear you. Over."

"Oh, thank God! We need immediate assistance. Our vehicle has broken down and we have a number of enemies approaching our position." He reeled off a set of coordinates that meant nothing to me. I quickly scribbled them down on the notepad next to the radio. *"Please,"* he added after giving me the coordinates. *"We need help."*

I opened the bridge door and leaned out, looking over at the *Lucky Escape*. Sam and Tanya were both on the sundeck, soaking up the sun. I called over to them. "Hey, someone's in trouble."

Tanya turned her head towards me, shielding her eyes from the sun with her hand, even though she was wearing a pair of large sunglasses that covered most of her face. "We're in the middle of a zombie apocalypse, Alex. A lot of people are in trouble."

"No, I mean there's someone on the radio

asking for help." I seized the notebook and read out the coordinates. "Is that far from here?"

"Up on those cliffs," Sam said, pointing to the shore. The cliffs were vertical and rose at least three hundred feet from the sea. "There's no way we're gonna get up there."

He was right. Without a helicopter, we weren't going to get anywhere near Echo Six. The radio squawked again and now the soldier's voice sounded even more desperate. *"If the person I was talking to is still there, please respond. We need your help. Can you hear me? Over."*

I hesitated, my thumb hovering over the Talk button. I didn't have the heart to tell this guy that there was no way I could help him, that his cry for help was futile. I wondered for a moment if I should tell him we were on our way but a false sense of hope might be just as bad as no hope at all. If I told these soldiers that we were coming to help them, they'd eventually realise it wasn't true. What if their last moments alive were spent dealing with the crushing knowledge that they'd been lied to?

I pressed the Talk button, then released it again. What should I say? I pressed the button again and then let it go for a second time. I didn't have the words. I couldn't tell these people that I wasn't going to help them.

The soldier's voice came through the static.

He sounded a little calmer. Maybe he was resigned to his fate, as his companion seemed to be. *"What's your name?"* he asked calmly.

He knew I was here and that I was hesitating. Each time I'd pressed the Talk button and released it without speaking, he would have heard a telltale *click* on his end.

"Alex," I said, trying to keep my voice flat but doing a bad job of it. I was trembling.

"Alex, listen carefully. My name is Sergeant Terry Locke. My team and I are in a broken-down army Land Rover at the coordinates I gave you. We're armed but the amount of zombies advancing on our position is too great. Our ammunition will soon be depleted. We're going down, Alex."

In the background, I could hear gunshots and someone shouting, *"Take that, you undead fuckers!"*

My grip on the radio tightened; these might be Sergeant Terry Locke's last words. I didn't want to hear him and his team get ripped apart by zombies.

"I'm going to tell you something very important, Alex," Sergeant Locke continued. *"There are items in this Land Rover that need to get to Doctor Sarah Ives at Bunker 53. It is vitally important that these items reach her. Do you copy?"*

"I...I don't know where Bunker 53 is," I told him.

"There's a map in the vehicle." He raised his

voice as the automatic gunfire around him increased in intensity. *"Listen carefully, Alex. These items are more important than any of us. My mission ends here but you need to continue it. The fate of what's left of the world may depend on it. Over."*

"All right," I said, determined to help. If I couldn't save Sergeant Locke, at least I could take these items to the doctor he'd mentioned. "I'll find a way to get to your vehicle. It may take some time but I'll do it. Over."

"There isn't much time," he said. *"There's a squad of soldiers on our tail. Now that we've broken down, they'll reach this location fairly soon. They must not be allowed to retrieve the items from the Land Rover. If they do, our efforts were wasted and we will have died for nothing. Over."*

"What do you mean soldiers on your tail? I thought *you* were soldiers? Over."

"We are. But we went against our orders and stole these items from Camp Victor. We couldn't let them continue what they were doing. We tried to stop Operation Dead Ground. Don't let them get the items back. If Operation Dead Ground continues, it could mean the end of the human race." I heard a loud crash and a scream. *"This is it,"* the Sergeant said. *"Goodbye, Alex, and good luck. Over and out."*

The channel went dead and the radio transmitted only static.

2

"We have to help them," I said. The four of us were sitting at the table in the living area of the *Big Easy*; Lucy next to me, Sam and Tanya opposite us. I had called the meeting and told everyone about the radio transmission from Echo Six. It was now ten minutes since the radio had gone dead.

"Sounds like it's too late to help them," Sam said.

"But what about the items in their Land Rover? Sergeant Locke said if they fell into the wrong hands, the human race could be in danger."

"We have no idea what it is," Lucy said. "And retrieving it will be dangerous. Haven't we faced enough danger to last us a lifetime?"

I couldn't argue with that. Since the outbreak

of the virus that had torn our world apart, we'd fought zombies, soldiers, and Patient Zero. We'd risked our lives to get vaccines to military camps, and we'd fought our way inland to a radio station. We'd seen our fair share of trouble but did that mean we were supposed to stop fighting?

After seeing my dad and brother cowering in a survivors camp, I'd made a pledge to not be like them, to stand up and fight against the zombies whenever I had to.

"We can't just ignore this," I said. "What if the items in the Land Rover really could destroy everyone? Whatever Operation Dead Ground is, it doesn't sound good. The clue is in the name. Sergeant Locke and his team were willing to risk court marshall and even death to stop it."

"Alex is right," Tanya said. "The Land Rover and whatever's inside it is sitting just up there on those cliffs. And a group of soldiers—maybe bad soldiers—want to get their hands on it. I'm willing to grab this item before they do and screw up their plans."

"But what makes you think this situation is survivable?" Lucy asked. "If the Echo Six team got killed by nasties, why do you think we'll fare any better?"

"They were trapped inside their vehicle," I told her. "It sounds like their Land Rover broke down and then they suddenly had a swarm of zombies surrounding them. They were immobilised. We won't have that disadvantage."

"We can find a car," Tanya said. "That way, we'll be able to keep moving while we engage the nasties. We might even be able to lead them away from the Land Rover and then double back when it's safer."

"So we're agreed?" I asked, looking at Lucy. "We'll do it?"

She shrugged and said flatly, "Sure, why not?" Her heart didn't seem in it but at least she'd acquiesced.

"So how are we going to get on top of the cliffs?' I asked, looking at Tanya and Sam for answers. If anyone knew about rock climbing, it was those two. But we didn't have any climbing gear and even if we did, I couldn't see myself scaling those cliffs. I'd probably die half way up, either from exhaustion or vertigo.

"We don't need to climb the cliffs," Tanya said. "There's a village with a harbour a few miles north of here. We get ashore, hotwire a car, and drive to the location the soldier gave you. Simple."

We all looked at each other. The village was probably going to be infested with zombies; it wasn't going to be *that* simple.

"Sounds like a plan," Sam said.

I couldn't think of any other way we were

going to get to the broken-down Land Rover so I nodded. “Sure, let’s do it.”

Lucy sighed. “Yeah, whatever.”

“You can stay with the boats if you like, Lucy,” Tanya said. “There’s no need for all four of us to go.”

“You can both stay,” Sam suggested. “Tanya and I will handle this.”

“No way,” I said. “I’m coming. I’m the one who answered the call.” I knew this mission was going to be dangerous but I felt that if I didn’t go to the Land Rover personally, as I’d promised Sergeant Locke I would, I’d be letting him and his team down.

“Okay, man,” Sam said, holding his hands up in mock surrender. “You can come too.”

“I’ll wait with the boats,” Lucy offered.

“Great,” Sam said. “Let’s head north and find the harbour.”

~

Five minutes later, I was sitting on the Zodiac with Sam and Tanya. Sam was in the stern, using the outboard motor’s tiller to steer us towards a small harbour in the distance. Tanya was kneeling in the bow, scanning the shoreline through a pair of binoculars.

Sitting on the floor by Sam’s feet was a small

box known as a Magpie. Military drones patrolled the coast and they'd take out any vehicle or personnel they detected. The Magpie emitted a signal which told the drones we were friendly.

As we sped across the water, cold salty spray flew into my face. I turned my head so I was looking behind us and I saw the *Big Easy* and *Lucky Escape* sitting out in deeper water. Lucy stood leaning on the *Big Easy*'s railings, watching the Zodiac cut through the sea towards land. From this distance, I couldn't see her face but I was sure her gaze was expressionless.

Sam saw me looking back the way we'd come and shouted so I could hear him above the splashing water and the growl of the motor. "Don't worry about her, man, she'll be fine."

"It isn't that," I told him. "It's just that she was really down on us helping those soldiers. That isn't like her at all."

He shrugged. "She's been through a lot, man. We all have. She's allowed to feel down whenever she wants."

I nodded. "Yeah, of course." I didn't expect Lucy to be happy all the time—given the circumstances we found ourselves in, it was a miracle we found any moments of happiness at all—but I was worried that she was isolating herself from the reality of our situation.

Whenever going ashore was mentioned, whether for a food run or to help someone like the soldiers who had called us on the radio, she became cold.

I didn't know if it was because each time we went ashore we might never return or if she was trying to forget what was happening on the mainland and focus her thoughts only on the relatively comfortable and safe world of the boat.

If that was the case, I really couldn't blame her; we all wanted to feel safe and the boat was the perfect haven from the zombie-infested mainland. But I found it impossible to remain in the bubble of protection afforded by the *Big Easy* when I knew someone needed help. Maybe that was where Lucy and I differed; she could ignore a cry for help where I could not.

"There's no movement on the shore," Tanya said, still peering through the binoculars. "And we'll get a choice of vehicle; I can see plenty of cars parked near the harbour. No boats, though. They were probably used to get everyone from the village to safety."

"Things are looking good so far," Sam said, ever the optimist. He throttled down as we got closer to the harbour and guided the Zodiac to the wooden jetty.

Tanya grabbed the mooring rope and jumped onto the jetty before securing the Zodiac to a cleat. I picked up the duffel bag of weapons from between my feet and tossed it to her. Then, followed closely by Sam, I climbed out of the boat and onto the wooden planks of the jetty.

Opening the bag, Tanya selected a Walther PPK handgun and an M16 rifle, which she slung over her shoulder. Sam and I did the same. The weapons were courtesy of the government when they'd recruited us to deliver vials of vaccine to a number of army bases and had come in handy on a number of occasions. The only problem was, we were running low on ammo.

In consideration of this fact, we'd also brought three baseball bats with us. In close quarters, they were just as useful as a gun. Actually, they were our weapon of choice because they didn't make any noise. A gunshot would attract zombies from miles around.

Brandishing a bat each, we left the empty duffel bag on the jetty and walked slowly and carefully to the shore. Tanya hadn't seen any obvious movement through the binoculars but that didn't mean someone couldn't be hiding in one of the buildings nearby or that there wasn't a horde of zombies around here, standing dormant until they heard a sound.

"This place is creepy," I whispered. "It's like a ghost town."

The road from the harbour climbed the cliff

and was bordered by a number of houses but all of them seemed empty. A small car park near where we stood was full of cars. This was probably the place where the residents parked their vehicles since there wasn't any space on the narrow road outside the houses.

"They definitely didn't drive out of here," Tanya said. "Maybe they all sailed away."

"Or the army took them," I said. Since the apocalypse had begun, the army seemed hellbent on rounding up all the survivors and placing them in military camps. They even used a government-run radio station, Survivor Radio, which urged everyone to go to their nearest camp.

My dad and brother were in one of those camps but I had no desire to join them. The last place I wanted to be was trapped behind walls and fences, reliant on the military to protect me from the nasties.

At least out here, I could choose my own destiny and even help others when the opportunity arose. It was a far cry from my former life as a nerdy gamer working a dead-end job and living off fast food.

We reached the cars and Sam pointed at a silver Nissan X-trail. He went over to it and tried the driver's door. It opened. Sam leaned inside and gave us a thumbs up. "The keys are inside."

"I guess the owners knew they weren't coming back," Tanya said, moving around to the passenger side.

I got in behind Sam and placed my weapons beside me on the back seat.

He started the engine and inspected the gauges on the dashboard. "Half a tank of petrol. More than enough for our needs." He put the vehicle into reverse and backed out of the parking space, spinning the steering wheel so we pointed in the direction of the road.

Tanya took a map out of her pocket and opened it. She pointed at it and said to Sam, "We're here." She traced her finger along the paper and stopped at an area she'd circled with a red pen. "We need to get to here."

"No problem." Sam put the X-Trail into gear and drove steadily to the car park's exit. Then he turned onto the road that wound past the houses and up to the top of the cliffs.

As we rolled past the houses, I watched their windows for signs of life. Or maybe 'signs of movement' would be a better term since life wasn't required for something to be moving in those buildings now that the apocalypse was here.

After seeing nothing behind the windows, I sat back in my seat and relaxed a little. The village appeared to be completely deserted.

"How long until we get to the Land Rover?" I asked.

"A couple of minutes," Tanya said. "It isn't far."

I felt a mounting sense of anticipation and fear. We knew the Land Rover had been attacked by zombies. Those same zombies would still be hanging around. And more would be arriving, attracted by the sound of gunfire.

Not to mention the soldiers Sergeant Locke had warned me of. They would also be on their way to the area. We were driving into a hotbed of activity.

We reached the clifftop. The road levelled out and then intersected a larger, main road. Sam turned left and we drove south. This road was lined with low dry stone walls and beyond them, I could see fields. In the distance, figures moved through the grass with slow, stumbling gaits. They were zombies and they were also moving south.

A couple of minutes later, I was jerked forward against my seatbelt when Sam hit the brakes suddenly.

"Looks like this is the place," he said.

The road ahead was crowded with shambling zombies. They seemed to have got onto the road by pushing through the dry stone walls because there were stones everywhere and the walls were destroyed. I guessed that this pack of creatures had been wandering in the fields when Echo Six's Land Rover had broken down. It had probably only taken a couple of minutes for the undead to stagger onto the road and surround the vehicle.

I could see Echo Six's Land Rover in the middle of the horde. The tailgate was open but no gunfire issued from the vehicle so I assumed everyone inside was dead.

Almost in unison, the zombies turned to face our vehicle. Their skin was the mottled grey-blue of dead flesh and the whites of their eyes had turned yellow. Many of them bore wounds that told the tale of their manner of death. Some had missing limbs, others deep scratches that had ripped their flesh apart.

Their clothes were ragged and torn, probably as a result of the undead corpses wandering around the countryside without regard for obstacles in their path.

"If I reverse back along the road," Sam said, "maybe I can lead them away from the Land Rov—"

His words were cut off and I leaned forward to see what had made him stop talking mid-sentence. Through the windscreen, I saw the zombies shambling towards us but nothing more.

Then I realised Sam was looking in the rearview mirror. I turned in my seat and saw two military Land Rovers behind us on the road.

These must be the soldiers Sergeant Locke had mentioned, the ones he warned must not get their hands on whatever it was Echo Six had stolen from them.

"There's no going back now," Sam said.

3

Instead of backing up, Sam slammed the gear stick into first gear and pressed the accelerator pedal gently. the X-Trail crept towards the zombie horde.

"Hold on," Sam said. "I'm going to try and bully my way through." He increased our speed slightly, keeping the vehicle in first gear. The zombies in front of the car didn't move so Sam simply plowed into them. Their bodies made sickening crunching sounds as they hit the radiator grill or went down beneath the tyres.

Undead hands slammed against the windows as the zombies who weren't in our path tried to force their way into the car. I peered out of my window at dozens of faces staring back at me with hateful yellow eyes. They wanted nothing more than to break my window, pull me out of the vehicle and rip me apart with their teeth and nails.

The hatred in their eyes sent a chill rushing along my spine.

I directed my attention to the two army Land Rovers behind us. They didn't move forward. Instead, they sat on the road, engines idling, waiting for something.

"They're not even shooting at us," I said.

Tanya turned in her seat and looked out of the rear window. "They don't know who we are and they have no idea Echo Six contacted us. As far as they know, we're just a group of civilians out on a day trip."

I thought about that. If the soldiers didn't know who we were, that gave us the element of surprise. They didn't know we were here for the contents of Echo Six's Land Rover so maybe we could use that to our advantage.

"What's the plan?" I asked the others.

"First we need to get through this horde of walking corpses," Sam said. "Then we need to either take out those soldiers behind us or get to the stuff in the Land Rover before they do and escape without getting shot."

He sped up slightly. We were moving at a speed slow enough to not plow into the zombies ahead of us at high speed and damage the car but fast enough that they couldn't break their way into the vehicle. That was a luxury Sergeant Locke and his team hadn't had. It was clear from the state of their Land Rover—which we were passing now—that the nasties had broken their way inside.

All of the windows were smashed and the tailgate was open. I tried to see inside the back of the vehicle but my view was blocked by zombies clawing at my window.

"I guess the guys inside will be hybrids now," Sam said.

The military had run a vaccination project to protect their personnel from becoming zombies if they got bitten. It had backfired spectacularly. If a vaccinated soldier was bitten by a zombie, instead of becoming undead, he would isolate himself for three or four days. This was an incubation period during which some sort of metamorphosis occurred.

After the incubation period, the soldier became a hybrid. Hybrids weren't animated dead corpses at all; they were much more dangerous. They were fast and strong and consumed by a murderous rage. Because they were alive and not made up of dead flesh, they didn't avoid rain or water or anything else. They were savage killing machines.

"They will be soon," I said, thinking of Sergeant Locke's voice on the radio. He'd trusted me to do what was right and now, thanks to a simple bite, he was turning into a monster much worse than he could ever have imagined.

We drove past the Land Rover and Sam increased our speed, taking us past the horde and onto clear road. Some of the zombies staggered after us but most turned their attention to the other two Land Rovers.

A group of six soldiers dressed in camouflage jackets and brandishing SA80 rifles were getting out of the vehicles and assuming firing stances. "Keep going," I told Sam. "They're going to start firing."

Sam floored the accelerator and the X-Trail sped along the road. As we drove around a sharp bend and the zombies and soldiers disappeared from view, I heard gunshots.

Sam hit the brakes and we came to a stop. He turned in his seat and looked at both me and Tanya. "What are we going to do? They'll kill the zombies and get the prize."

"I don't know," I said. "I saw eight soldiers. Three got out of each Land Rover and the drivers stayed inside."

"Eight of them, three of us," Tanya said. "I don't like those odds."

It wasn't only the odds I didn't like. Those soldiers back there were human beings, just like us. Dispatching zombies and killing hybrids was one thing but taking the lives of men who were probably just following orders was something else entirely.

I cursed the fact that we'd wasted so much time on the *Big Easy* debating whether or not to come ashore. If we'd arrived here before the soldiers, we could have taken out the zombies and be long gone by now but their presence made things a lot more complicated.

"So what do we do?" Sam asked again. "I'm not going home until I know what's in that Land Rover that's so important."

"Agreed," I said. I'd promised Sergeant Locke I'd help and I wasn't about to give up and go home. But I also didn't want innocent blood on my hands.

Tanya was studying the map. She showed it to Sam and said, "If we follow this road and take the next left, it'll take us to this crossroads here." She pointed at a spot on the map. "Assuming they're going to return the same way they came, we can set up an ambush."

"Sounds good," Sam said, putting the car back into gear and setting off again. "They deal with the zombies while we wait. Then we take the mystery box from them while they're transporting it back to their base. Sounds easy."

I leaned forward in my seat. "Easy? Those men back there are trained soldiers. If we get in a firefight with them, I don't like the odds, whether we ambush them or not. And should we even be trying to kill them in the first place? They're probably innocent military personnel following orders from someone higher up the chain of command."

Sam frowned at me in the rearview mirror. "Dude, you're the one who said they're evil."

"I never said they're evil."

He looked at Tanya. "Did he say they're evil?"

"Not exactly."

Turning his attention back to me, he said, "Well if they're not evil, we should just let them take whatever's in that Land Rover back to their base so they can continue Operation Dead Ground. Because that definitely doesn't sound evil to me, dude. Sounds to me like they're trying to save the human race with a name like that."

"Turn here," Tanya told him.

He turned left and we were heading north again, on a road that ran parallel to the one we'd just been on.

"So we're going to ambush and kill them?" I asked. It didn't feel right to me that we were planning to murder these soldiers just to get whatever they were taking from Echo Six's Land Rover.

"Do you have a better plan, Alex?" Tanya asked.

I tried to think of something—*anything*—that would mean we could recover the items from the soldiers without any loss of life but nothing came to mind. Where Sam, Tanya, and Lucy were the gung-ho action heroes of our group, I was usually the planner, the thinker, the ideas guy. But right now, I felt totally useless.

Staring out of the window, I wondered if I could aim my gun at an innocent man and pull the trigger. The fields of grass undulating in the slight breeze and the distant shimmering sea had no answers for me so I turned away from the window and focused on my two companions.

Tanya was studying the map with emotionless dark eyes and Sam was staring at the road ahead.

"Hey," he said, catching my eyes in the rearview mirror, "We've had run-ins with the military before and you've fired a few shots. Why is this time different?"

"Those other times, it was self-defence."

"So think of this as self-defence as well. If that guy on the radio was right, there's some bad shit in that Land Rover and those evil soldiers are going to take it back to their base where it's probably going to be used to end the world or something."

"I didn't say they were evil," I reminded him.

He threw his hands up for a moment before returning them to the steering wheel. "Whatever, man. The point is, stopping these soldiers is self-defence against whatever shit they're going to pull with the items on that Land Rover. And we're not only defending ourselves; we're defending the world."

I sat back in my seat and let out a long sigh. I wished Sergeant Locke had given me more information about what his team had stolen from Camp Victor. As it was, we were simply taking him at his word. What if we had it wrong?

"What if Echo Six were the evil soldiers?" I said. "What if they stole something that the guys at Camp Victor were using for good? We might be about to kill the good guys." But even as I said the words, they rang hollow. Locke had told me the items needed to get to somewhere called Bunker 53. That sounded like a government installation to me. If Locke and his team were trying to disrupt military operations, they wouldn't be trying to get whatever they stole to the government unless they thought that what they were doing was right and they were trying to warn the people in authority about Operation Dead Ground.

"Come on, man," Sam said. "We all know that doesn't make sense."

"Alex," Tanya said, turning to face me. "We need you to be with us on this. The ambush isn't going to be easy. We need to be at the top of our game, okay?"

"Yeah," I said, nodding. "Okay."

"And don't forget, you're the one who dragged us here," Sam reminded me. "So don't wimp out on us now."

"I won't," I told him. "Don't worry about me, I'm one hundred per cent on board with the plan."

"Turn left here," Tanya told Sam. "The crossroads is just ahead."

He turned the car and I saw the four-way intersection in the distance. This was it. This was where it was all going to go down.

4

Sam brought the X-trail to a halt before we reached the crossroads and got out, surveying the area with his hands on his hips.

I opened my door and slid out. The day was really warming up now and I felt the sun burning my skin even after only a couple of minutes exposure. I reminded myself to get plenty of sunscreen the next time we went on a supply run.

If there was a next time.

"Any ideas?" Sam asked Tanya.

She nodded and pointed at a field on the other side of the crossroads. "If we get someone set up in that field over there and someone in this field here, we can create a crossfire with the enemy Land Rovers in the middle."

"How do we make sure they don't just drive away?" Sam asked.

"We use the X-Trail to block the road."

"I'm not so sure that will work," I said. "As soon as they see the X-Trail blocking their way, they'll probably suspect something's up and turn around."

"Do you have a better idea?" she asked me.

I nodded. "Yeah, but it's risky. Someone needs to wait on this road in the X-Trail. As the Land Rovers are about to reach the crossroads, that person needs to drive the X-Trail into their path. By the time the drivers react, the two people stationed in the fields will have the vehicles in their crosshairs."

"Sounds good, man," Sam said. "So who volunteers to be the driver?"

"I'll do it," I said. "You two are the best shots anyway. I'll make sure they stop and then you and Tanya open fire."

"You're going to have to act quickly," Tanya said. "And once you've blocked the road, you need to take out the driver of the lead vehicle, as well as anyone else sitting in the front seat. You'll be putting yourself directly into their line of fire so they offer the most danger to you."

Suddenly, driving the car didn't seem like the best job after all.

Tanya looked at the road along which the Land Rovers would be approaching. "We need to get into position. It may take them some time to deal with the zombies and load the items from Echo Six's Land Rover into their own but we can't afford to be caught out. We need to be ready for them."

"I'll take the far field," Sam said. "I should be able to get into position behind the wall."

"And I'll set up in this field," Tanya said. "If I position myself a little farther back along the road, I should be able to make sure the rear Rover can't escape by reversing and I won't be directly across the road from you, which could be dangerous."

"Yeah, we don't want to shoot each other, man." Sam turned to me. "You know what you're doing, right?"

I nodded. "Yeah, don't worry about my end. I've got it covered."

"Good man." He grabbed his weapons and set off towards the field across the road. Tanya did the same and climbed over the stone wall by the side of the road. She waded through the long grass as she looked for an ideal hiding spot.

Shielding my eyes from the sun, I watched them as they found their positions and ducked down below the stone wall that lined the road the Land Rovers would be coming along.

I climbed into the X-Trail and dialled the air conditioning up to max. The vents blasted frigid air over me and I tried to imagine that the icy blast was freezing my emotions and making me into a cold-hearted killer. After all, that was what I was about to become, wasn't it?

I sat there in the cold air for at least five minutes before I saw the sun flash off something on the road to my right. Squinting my eyes, I could make out two Land Rovers in the distance, heading this way.

I took the handbrake off and put the X-Trail into first gear, keeping my foot on the clutch so the vehicle didn't move just yet. I couldn't see Sam or Tanya now—they were too well-hidden in the long grass behind the walls—but I was sure they'd be able to hear the deep growl of the army Land Rovers' engines as they got closer.

The distance between me and the crossroads wasn't far and it would take no more than a few seconds to cover but I had to wait until the right moment and arrive there an instant before the other vehicles. Then I had to start firing. The M16 and Walther PPK lay on the passenger seat next to me, within easy reach.

I pressed the button that lowered my window. When the glass had buzzed all the way down, I could hear the Land Rovers approaching.

I tightened my grip on the steering wheel. My hands were shaking. So much could go wrong in the next few minutes. We could all end up dead. I tried to push that thought out of my head but it clung to my brain and kept repeating itself over and over.

Forcing out a breath, I forced myself to raise the clutch slowly and steadily. If I let it up too fast and stalled the car, all was lost.

The X-Trail inched forward.

I released the clutch fully and crawled toward the crossroads in first gear, ready to press the accelerator when the Land Rovers got closer and pick up speed.

The military vehicles were moving quite quickly for such a narrow road. I guessed their speed to be around fifty miles-per-hour.

I waited as long as I dared before putting my foot down and racing for the crossroads.

Somehow, I timed the maneuver perfectly and arrived at the four-way intersection moments before the Land Rovers. I hit the brakes and skidded to a stop, blocking their path.

The driver in the lead vehicle saw me and his eyes went wide. He slammed on the brakes but the Land Rover had been going so fast that he couldn't stop it in time. A high-pitched squealing filled the air as the Rover's tyres skidded on the road. Through my open window, I saw the vehicle grow larger and larger as it got closer.

Then it hit the X-Trail and my door caved in with a sickening metallic *crunch*. I reached for the M16, intending to spray bullets through my open window, but the soldier sitting next to the driver had figured out that this collision had been no mere accident and had raised his weapon and aimed it at me.

Throwing myself across the passenger seat, I heard bullets hiss through the air over my head. They penetrated the passenger side window and a couple embedded themselves in the pillar that held the windscreen in place.

I scrambled across the seat and opened the passenger door, sliding out headfirst onto the road. The air was filled with the sound of gunfire now. Sam and Tanya must have opened fire on the vehicles and the soldiers were firing back.

I raised my head to peek over the X-Trail's bonnet at the lead Land Rover. All of its doors were open and there were no soldiers inside. The guy who had been shooting at me and the driver had either been caught in the crossfire or were coming this way.

Crouching low, I made my way to the rear of the X-Trail and peered around the tailgate. The soldier who'd shot at me was standing there, gun in hand. He'd obviously planned to surprise me but my sudden appearance had taken him off guard.

His eyes went wide and he brought his weapon up.

I squeezed the M16's trigger and sprayed the

soldier's chest with bullets. They *thwacked* through his combat jacket and red mist filled the air in front of him. He dropped straight away, his SA80 clattering onto the road.

I didn't have time to retrieve it; or even to make sure the soldier was dead; the driver was still around somewhere. I crept back behind the X-Trail, keeping the M16 pointed ahead of me in case anyone else should suddenly appear in my sights.

Despite the sound of gunfire and shouts coming from the area around the Land Rovers, I could hear light footfalls on the other side of the X-Trail. The soldier—the one who'd been driving the lead Rover—was trying to sneak up on me.

Freezing so I wouldn't make any footsteps of my own, I raised the muzzle of the M16 and waited for my stalker to come into view around the front of the car. The footsteps stopped. I tried to slow my breathing in case it was giving away my position.

When he came around the car, he didn't appear where I expected him to be. Instead of coming on foot, he rolled from behind the front tyre, aiming a handgun at me. He managed to fire before I did but because he was rolling, his aim was off and the bullet thwacked into the side of the X-Trail.

I took aim and squeezed the M16's trigger.

When the momentum of his roll was spent and his body came to a stop, he lay face down on the road, forehead on the asphalt and eyes closed.

As a precautionary measure, I kicked the handgun away and nudged him with the sole of my boot. He didn't move. He'd never move again.

The gunshots had died down now and the air was thick with the smell of spent ammo and hot metal. I had no idea what had happened at the Land Rovers. For all I knew, Sam and Tanya were dead and the remaining soldiers were closing in on my position.

I raised my head above the bonnet of the X-Trail and checked out the situation. The Land Rovers were riddled with bullet holes. Glass and dead bodies lay scattered around the vehicles. I counted six dead soldiers. Along with the two I'd killed, that made eight. Unless anyone was hiding within the Rovers, we'd taken out the military unit with our ambush.

But at what cost?

I shouted out to my companions, my voice breaking the silence that had descended upon the area like a shroud. "Sam? Tanya?"

I saw Tanya vaulting over the wall at the side of the road. She approached the Land Rovers slowly and carefully, her M16 raised, and peered into the rear of the vehicles. Then she lowered her weapon and shouted, "Clear!"

Sam's head appeared above the wall on the other side of the road. His lips were drawn back in a wide grin and his eyes looked a little wild. He climbed over the wall and strode up to the Land Rovers. "Man, that was a blast!"

I didn't share his enthusiasm. We'd just killed eight people. I only hoped it was worth it.

Sam clapped a hand across my back when I joined him and Tanya at the rear Land Rover. "Good job, Alex! You timed that crash perfectly."

"Not so perfectly," I told him. "They crashed into me. The X-Trail is pretty beaten up."

He shrugged. "Hey, don't worry about it, man. There are plenty more cars where that came from."

"True," I said. "But we still need to get back to the boats somehow."

He looked over at the X-Trail and for a moment his face fell. "You mean it's wrecked?"

It was my turn to shrug. "I don't know. They hit it pretty hard and the engine died."

"We'll find away back to the boats," Tanya said. "Even if we have to take one of the Land Rovers."

"The problem with that," I said, "is that they might have trackers fitted to them. The bad guys might know where we are."

"We'll worry about that later." Sam climbed into the back of the Land Rover. "Let's see what the hell is so valuable that everyone is willing to die for it." He looked around the dark interior of the vehicle and sounded disappointed when he said, "Nothing. There's nothing in here."

"There were four soldiers in the back of this Rover," Tanya said. "It was only used for transporting personnel. I think the good stuff is in the lead vehicle."

We went to the other vehicle and peered into the back. The first thing I noticed was a steel crate that must have been at least six feet long. It was locked with a padlock and had no external markings that might reveal its contents.

Next to the crate sat a drab green military footlocker. It was also padlocked.

"The keys have to be around here somewhere," Tanya said. She went to the front of the Land Rover and leaned inside. She came back and opened her hand. Two small keys lay in her palm. "They were sitting on the dashboard," she said.

"Should we open them up here or wait until we get back to the boats?" I said, aware that the eight soldiers lying dead on the road might have been part of a larger unit.

"I'm not waiting, man," Sam said, taking the keys from Tanya's hand and climbing into the back of the Land Rover. He went to the crate first and unlocked the padlock before pushing the lid open.

Looking inside, he frowned. "There's a lot of packing material." He pulled out blankets and bubble wrap, piling them behind him on the Land Rover's floor.

Echo Six must have packed these items into the crate to protect whatever was inside during the journey to Bunker 53.

Sam stopped pulling out the packing materials suddenly and his face became worried. "Shit. Guys, you've got to see this."

Tanya and I climbed into the Land Rover and looked into the crate.

Lying at the bottom of the crate was a man's body that had been vacuum-packed inside a bag made of thick, clear plastic. When I saw the dead man's face, my breath caught in my throat.

A month ago, we'd buried this body in a deep grave up on the cliffs, hoping no one would ever find it.

It was the body of Dr Marcus Vess.

Patient Zero.

5

"We buried this fucker a month ago," Sam said. "How did he get here?"

"Someone must have dug him up," I offered. It was the only explanation for Vess's body being in the back of this Land Rover. The military had found the grave and exhumed Vess.

"Patient Zero," Tanya said. "What do the military want with Patient Zero?"

Years of reading about conspiracy theories gave me the answer to that question. "They're obviously trying to weaponise the virus."

"But he doesn't have the virus inside him anymore, man," Sam said. "You shot him full of vaccine, remember? It killed him."

"I remember. But look closely. When I injected the vaccine into him, the dark veins in his skin disappeared and the yellowness in his eyes faded. The veins in his neck and arms look darker now. Not as dark as they had been when he was alive but definitely darker than normal. And look at his eyes." Vess's eyes were open, staring at us through the thick plastic. "Some of the yellowness has returned around the edges."

Sam pushed himself away from the crate. "You mean he's coming back to life?"

"No, I'm not saying that. But it's obvious that the virus is still alive in his body. He has the purest form of the virus in his body because he injected himself with it and that's what started all this craziness. Anyone else who has the virus inside them—the zombies and the hybrids—has a diluted form that's been passed on by a bite or a scratch. If the military want to weaponise the virus in some way, Vess's body is a good place to get samples of blood and tissue."

"You think that's what's been happening?" Sam asked. "They've been dissecting him?"

"Probably not dissecting him. He looks pretty much intact. But they've probably been taking his blood and experimenting with it."

Sam shook his head as if in disbelief. "That shit is fucked up, man."

"Wait a minute," Tanya said. "Are you sure he isn't going to come back to life? If the vaccine killed him but the virus is fighting the vaccine, who's to say he won't just wake up once the virus becomes strong enough?"

"The vaccine didn't kill him," I reminded her. "Those four bullets did." I pointed to the four holes in Vess's chest. Our friend Johnny Drake had shot Vess but the virus had protected Vess from the bullets. "When the vaccine suppressed the virus, its protective properties disappeared and the damage Vess's body had received from those bullets finally killed him."

"Yeah, I get that," she said. "But if the virus is getting stronger inside him, it might repair the damaged tissue or something. I don't know, I'm no scientist. But I do know that we shouldn't take any chances."

"Yeah," Sam said, closing the lid of the metal crate and locking the padlock. "I agree with Tanya."

"Fine," I said. "Let's get the body to Bunker 53 as fast as we can."

Sam threw his arms in the air helplessly. "That'd be great, man. If we knew where Bunker 53 is."

I pointed at the footlocker. "Why not take a look in there? There might be a map or something."

He looked at the footlocker as if suddenly

remembering it was there. "Oh, yeah." Using the other key, he unlocked it and lifted the lid. "There's lot of stuff in here. Papers and notebooks mostly."

"We need to take it all with us," I said.

I heard a sound in the distance and tried to discern exactly what it was.

Tanya beat me to it. "Vehicles. Coming this way."

"Shit!" Sam closed the footlocker. "We need to get this stuff loaded into the X-Trail."

"There's no time for that." I slid out of the back of the Land Rover and onto the road. "We need to get out of here now." It sounded like there were at least half a dozen vehicles heading this way. If we were still here when they arrived, we'd end up dead.

"I'll drive." Tanya vaulted out of the Land Rover and went around to the driver's door. She opened it and slid inside.

"I'll get the X-Trail out of the way," I said, running to the Nissan and leaning in through the passenger door to take the handbrake off. I braced myself against the door pillar and pushed the car towards the side of the road. Sam joined me and pushed from the back. We managed to get the car out of the Land Rover's way.

I ran to the passenger side and got in next to

Tanya. Sam, standing in the road, looked disappointed. "Where am I supposed to sit?"

"In the back," Tanya suggested.

"With Patient Zero?" A fearful expression crossed his face. "Fuck that. I'll follow in the other Land Rover."

"Fine." Tanya put our Rover into gear and started along the road.

In the side mirror, I watched Sam dash to the Rover behind us and climb behind the wheel. The vehicle roared as he revved the engine, then fell into place directly behind us as we drove across the crossroads and headed north.

"How far away do you think those other vehicles are?" I asked Tanya.

She shrugged. "I can't see them in the rearview but they can't be that far behind us."

My mind ran over the logistics of what we needed to do to escape with our lives and our prize. Somehow, we had to unload the crate containing Vess and the footlocker from the Land Rover into the Zodiac. Then we had to load them from the Zodiac onto the *Big Easy* or the *Lucky Escape*. The soldiers following us would have a clear shot at us the whole time and they'd know about our boats.

If they didn't manage to kill us during the unloading and loading process, the soldiers would probably call in an air strike or something.

After all, there were drones patrolling the entire coastline and it would probably be easy to send one in our direction.

"We can't go back to the boats," I told Tanya. "They'll know where we are and blow us out of the water."

"I already figured that out," she told me. "I'm not heading for the boats. Not while these jokers are on our tail, anyway."

"So where are we going?"

"Anywhere but the coast."

I felt a twinge of fear. Heading inland could be dangerous. If we came across a town or a city, that could mean facing hundreds or even thousands of zombies. It was also possible that we might unwittingly drive into an area where a large horde was waiting for prey like a thousand spiders waiting for an unwary fly to wander into their web.

Tanya pushed the map at me. "Find a route that will get us out of this area and also be clear of nasties."

She might as well have asked me to find the lost ark of the covenant. I had no idea which roads might be safe and which might be crawling with zombies.

I found our location on the map and glanced over the surrounding area. There was a motorway a little farther inland or we could stick to these country roads and continue north. At least if we got to the motorway, we could transfer our cargo to another vehicle. I was sure these Land Rovers had trackers installed and that meant we'd never get away from the military as long as we stayed in them.

"There's a motorway service station a bit further northwest," I said. "We should probably change vehicles and then double back."

Tanya nodded. "If we get to the motorway, we can pick up speed and outrun our pursuers. It's too hard to get any kind of speed on these narrow roads."

"A headstart should give us a chance to load the crate and footlocker into another car. If we're fast enough, we could be heading back south while the vehicles behind us are still heading north. Then we can get to the boats and load everything onto them safely."

"Sounds good," Tanya said. "How do we get to the motorway?"

I consulted the map. "Take the next left. Then you should see signs."

She slowed down for the turn and took it. I checked in the mirror to see if Sam was still following us. He was close behind and probably wondering where the hell we were going. There was still no sign of our pursuers, if that was what the other vehicles actually were. I opened my window and stuck my head out for a moment to see if I could still hear them but we were travelling too fast for me to hear anything other than the wind in my ears.

"The motorway's six miles ahead," Tanya said, pointing at a road sign. "Once we get onto it, how far is it to the services?"

I closed my window and studied the map. "I'm not sure exactly. Four or five miles, I think."

She nodded and put her foot down.

Less than ten minutes later, we crossed a bridge that stretched over the motorway. I looked down at the road below us and felt a flood of relief when I didn't see any vehicles on the the three lanes that headed north. The southbound carriageway was another story; the lanes were full of abandoned cars.

"Why wasn't anyone heading north?" Tanya asked, peering at the motorway.

"I have no idea," I said.

She turned onto a ramp that descended to the northbound lanes. Once we were on the motorway, I checked the mirror to see what was behind us. What I saw explained the lack of cars on this stretch of road. It looked like at least a dozen cars had been involved in an accident that had blocked the road. The cars south of our location hadn't been able to get past the pile up.

"That explains that," Tanya said, checking her mirror.

Sam came up alongside us and motioned for Tanya to wind down her window.

When she did so, he shouted, "Where are we going?"

"To ditch these vehicles," she shouted back. "There's a place up ahead."

He nodded. "Okay, sounds good."

"We'll double back and get to the boats," I shouted.

"Cool." He looked in his mirror and his face fell. "Guys, we have company."

I turned in my seat and checked behind us. Two big boxy-looking vehicles were crossing the bridge. They were painted a sand colour and looked like some sort of armoured personnel carriers. Following them was a long, similarly coloured six-wheeled vehicle. In a matter of minutes, they'd be behind us on the motorway.

"The two lead vehicles are Foxhounds," Sam shouted to us. "The one in the rear is a Jackal. They're all personnel carriers so I reckon there could be maybe twenty soldiers back there."

Sam obviously knew his military vehicles. All I knew about the sandy-coloured monstrosities behind us was that they looked dangerous.

"Right, let's get the hell out of here," Tanya said. She pressed the button that closed her window and put her foot down. We raced along the motorway.

"We should be able to outrun them," she said.

I watched the three vehicles begin their descent of the ramp and hoped she was right.

6

We raced along the empty motorway in the Land Rovers. Our pursuers were still visible in the mirrors but they were losing ground. They were probably burdened with the weight of passengers, equipment, and weapons whereas our vehicles were virtually unladen save for the crate containing Marcus Vess.

A blue sign at the side of the road told us that the services were just a mile ahead.

"We can't stop," Tanya said. "They're still too close behind us. By the time we find a suitable vehicle, they'll catch up with us."

I nodded. "Understood. But if we don't stop at the services, we're going to be forced to stop anyway." I pointed ahead. In the distance, every lane of the motorway was clogged with stationary cars. We were running out of clear road.

"Shit," Tanya muttered.

The slip road that led to the services appeared in front of us and she turned onto it. "We don't have a choice," she said as she decelerated.

We entered the car park. A lot of cars were parked here and we'd have our choice of vehicles if only we had more time.

Unfortunately, time was something we didn't have in abundance.

Tanya slowed our vehicle to a crawl and Sam drove up alongside us. "What's up?" he asked through his open window.

"We've run out of motorway," Tanya told him.

"Yeah, I saw that. And we don't have time to stop and switch cars."

Tanya nodded. "Exactly."

"So what are we going to do?"

"Maybe set up a defensive position in that building and keep them at bay?" Tanya suggested, pointing to the brick building which housed a KFC and a McDonalds.

"They'll just send for more reinforcements," I said. "Besides, the building is full of nasties." I could see them shambling behind the windows of the two-storey structure.

Sam pointed beyond the building to a wooden fence that served as the boundary between the services and a field. "What if we go off-road?"

Tanya looked in the direction he was pointing. "That'll work. We might be able to pick up a different road somewhere in that direction. Alex, check the map."

I did so. If we made it across the field, there was indeed a road on the other side. "Yeah," I said. "There's a road over there but we need to lose the soldiers on our tail and I have an idea how we can do that. Or at least slow them down."

"Okay," she said. "What is it?"

I pointed at the brick building. "If we release those zombies into the car park, they could cover our escape."

She nodded. "I like it. Let's do it." She drove over to the glass door that served as the entrance and exit for the building. It was probably an automatic door but someone had locked it. I grabbed my baseball bat and got out of the Land Rover.

When I reached the door, I peered inside. The lights were off so I couldn't see much but there was definitely movement inside; a furtive shambling in the shadows.

I swung the bat at the glass and created a spiderweb of cracks. A second swing shattered the panel and it crashed to the ground.

When the zombies inside came out of the

darkness and lurched towards the door, I realised just how many of them there were. A foul stench preceded them and I gagged against it. They'd been shut up in this building for God knew how long and the air was fetid.

"Come on!" Tanya shouted from the Land Rover.

I didn't need telling twice. I sprinted for the vehicle and climbed inside as the first nasties made their way through the shattered door and into the car park. They detected the noise of our cars and staggered towards us. Behind them, more of the undead stepped into the daylight.

"Jesus, how many of them are there?" Tanya asked.

"At least a hundred, I think."

She floored the accelerator and sped toward the edge of the car park before mounting the grass verge that led to the fence. We crashed through the wooden barricade and bounced along the rutted field, followed by Sam.

Behind us, more zombies poured out of the building and flooded the car park like a river of rotting flesh. The soldiers in the pursuing vehicles were going to have a hard time getting past them and hopefully by then we'd be long gone.

The ride across the field was rough and when

we got to the other side, we discovered a long hedge.

"The road is on the other side," I told Tanya.

She steered us towards the hedge and put her foot down. "Hold on."

We hit the hedge and ripped through it, hitting a narrow road on the other side. Tanya spun the steering wheel to the right and headed north. Sam missed the hole we'd created in the hedge and made his own, ending up on the road behind us. I turned in my seat to make sure he was okay and saw him grinning like the cat that got the cream. This was the kind of thing Sam lived for.

We drove along the road for twenty minutes before I saw a farmhouse on the left. I pointed it out to Tanya. "Could be a suitable vehicle there."

She nodded. "Let's take a look."

We had to find a vehicle soon or we'd be caught by the military. No matter how long we delayed them, if these Land Rovers had trackers fitted, they'd always be able to find us eventually.

The route to the farm consisted of a narrow dirt road with fields on either side. As we drove along it, I scanned the house ahead looking for signs of danger.

The place looked deathly quiet.

As well as the house, there was a barn and a row of outbuildings that looked like they might have once served as stables. Tanya parked in front of the house and we both got out. Sam came to a stop behind us and joined us. He was carrying his M16, as was Tanya. I had my Walther in one hand and the bat in the other.

"Looks quiet," Sam said.

We all knew that silence could be deceiving. Without any external stimuli, such as sound or movement, the zombies went into a state of dormancy and didn't move until they heard or saw prey. There could be a hundred of them in the area just waiting to detect movement.

The house's front door consisted of wood that had been painted bright yellow and a curtained glass panel. I noticed that the windows were also curtained.

There was no way of knowing if anyone—or anything—was inside and that wasn't our priority right now anyway because parked around the back of the house was a denim blue-coloured Volvo XC90. The seven-seater SUV had more than enough room to carry the crate that currently housed Patient Zero.

Same went over to the vehicle and looked in through the windows. "The keys are inside. Looks like someone left in a hurry and left it behind."

"Or they're still in the house," I said.

"Could be. As long as they don't come out, I

don't really care. Let's get this baby loaded up." He slid into the driver's seat and started the engine. After checking the gauges, he grinned. "More than enough fuel to get us to the boats."

"Okay, let's get everything onboard," Tanya said. "We're going to have to fold the rear seats down to get Vess in and someone's going to have to ride in the back with him."

"That someone is you, Alex," Sam said.

I let out a sigh. "Fine." I didn't really mind riding in the back but it might have been nice to have a democratic decision about it rather than me just being told what to do.

Tanya and I pulled the six foot long crate from the back of the Land Rover and, taking an end each, manoeuvred it to the Volvo while Sam folded the rear seats down. We slid the crate into the cargo area and I climbed in beside it.

Sam brought the footlocker over and placed it by my feet. Then he climbed behind the wheel and we set off back along the dirt track.

"That was easy enough," Tanya said from the passenger seat. She was consulting the map, which she'd unfolded and propped against the dashboard.

"We aren't out of the woods yet," I reminded her. "Those soldiers will be heading this way."

"Relax, man, we'll be long gone," Sam said.

"Take a left at the bottom of the track," Tanya

told him. "We'll head north for a while before finding another road that will take us back down south to the boats."

I leaned back against the metal crate and relaxed a little. The military vehicles would reach the farm soon but the soldiers would find the Land Rovers empty and they'd have no clue as to which direction we'd gone.

As soon as we got back to the boats, we could sail out into deeper water while we figured out where the hell Bunker 53 was located.

I opened the footlocker and checked out its contents. As Sam had said, it was filled with papers and journals. Somewhere in here, we'd hopefully find a piece of information that would tell us where we could find the bunker.

I hoped it wasn't too far away because I wanted to get rid of Patient Zero as soon as possible.

The more I thought about it, the more I realised that Sam had probably been right about Vess after all.

The virus was probably bringing him back to life.

7

We got back to the village an hour and a half later. Using the map, Tanya had taken us on a circuitous route to make sure our pursuers wouldn't chance upon us and that tactic had worked; we hadn't seen the military vehicles again since leaving the motorway.

As we drove down to the harbour, I felt a sense of relief when I saw the *Big Easy* and the *Lucky Escape* anchored just off shore. I couldn't see Lucy on deck but knew she was somewhere on the boat, probably waiting to tell us off for taking so long. I didn't mind; we'd made it back alive and that was all that really mattered.

Sam drove the Volvo onto the jetty and parked it right next to the Zodiac. Then the three of us loaded the crate and footlocker into the inflatable, along with the weapons.

Unfortunately, with the items on board, there wasn't enough room for all of us to get into the small boat.

"Someone's going to have to wait here," Sam said.

I got into the Zodiac. "Well it isn't going to be me." I folded my arms and kind of felt like a petulant child having a tantrum but I'd had enough of always being the member of the group who had to take the less-palatable option and I was desperate to get back on board the *Big Easy*.

Sam laughed. "No problem, dude. You don't have to have a fit about it. I'll stay."

"Great," Tanya said, getting into the Zodiac and throwing Sam his M16 before starting the outboard motor. "I'll come back to get you in a bit."

"No worries." Sam climbed up onto the Volvo's bonnet and lay back with his hands behind his head. He closed his eyes and said, "I'll be here catching some rays."

We cast off from the jetty and as we began moving forwards towards the boats, Tanya gestured to the metal crate. "Where are we going to store this?"

I shrugged. "I suppose we'll have to put it in one of the storerooms."

"We'll put it on the *Lucky Escape*," she said.

"But once it's in there, I'm locking the storeroom door."

I nodded slowly. "Yeah, I don't blame you."

She raised an eyebrow. "You think he might really come back to life? You told Sam he wouldn't."

"Yeah, but I've been thinking about it a bit more and I think it's possible. The virus is obviously still in his body and it seems to be reasserting control. Did you notice how his body hasn't decayed at all?"

"I thought that was because he's been shrink-wrapped."

"I think there's more to it than that." The truth was, we didn't really know enough about the virus to understand how it interacted with human hosts. Maybe the scientist Sergeant Locke had mentioned—Dr Sarah Ives—would know more. The sooner we found her, the better.

"We'll unload the footlocker onto the *Big Easy*," I suggested to Tanya. "I want to go through the papers and find out where the hell we can find Bunker 53. The sooner we take Vess there, the sooner he becomes someone else's problem and not ours."

"Sounds good to me."

We reached the *Lucky Escap*e and tied the Zodiac to the stern. Between us, we managed to manhandle the metal crate on board, although we had to tie ropes around the crate's handles to drag it up to the aft deck. I kept checking the *Big Easy* to see if Lucy would appear on deck but even the commotion we were making didn't bring her from belowdecks.

After dragging the crate into the storeroom and locking it in there, I said to Tanya, "Has Lucy told you she's feeling depressed or anything lately?"

She shook her head. "If she was going to confide in anyone, it would be you, Alex. You're closer to her than I am."

"Yeah, I guess so," I said uncertainly. Lucy and I had been close, there was no doubt about that, but she seemed to be pulling away from me lately, both physically and emotionally.

"If you're worried about her," Tanya said. "Why not have a talk with her while I go back to get Sam?"

I nodded. I wasn't really sure what I was going to say to Lucy.

Tanya must have seen the uncertainty on my face because she said, "Just ask her how she's doing."

"Yeah, I'll do that."

We got back into the Zodiac and Tanya helped me get the footlocker on board the *Big Easy* before she took the Zodiac back towards the harbour where I could see Sam still sunbathing on the Volvo's bonnet. I watched her and the Zodiac for a moment before leaving the footlocker on the deck and heading into the living area.

Survivor Radio was coming through the speakers in here. *The Clash* were playing *London Calling*. I went through the door that led belowdecks and called out Lucy's name. There was no answer.

I found her on the bed. She was curled up, facing the wall.

Sitting on the mattress next to her, I asked, "Are you okay?"

"Not really," she murmured.

"What's wrong?"

"It doesn't matter. There's nothing you can do to change it."

I put a hand on her shoulder. "Still, it might help to talk about it."

She sighed. "I've had enough."

"Enough of what?"

"Of everything. The fighting. The danger. The uncertainty. I can't take it anymore."

I felt helpless. What could I do to help her? The world had changed and the days when life seemed safe were gone. Now, everything was a fight for survival and danger lurked around every corner.

"We're safe on the boats," I offered. It was a

lame thing to say. Despite the relative safety of the boats compared to being on land, we had to make constant supply runs on land and every run we undertook put us in danger.

"We're not safe," Lucy said. "One day we'll run into pirates or the hybrids will learn to swim. Or the army will blow us out of the water."

"We'll just have to face those things if and when they happen," I told her.

"I don't want to face them. I want to feel safe again."

I didn't know what to say to that. There was nothing I could say or do to make her feel safe. I noticed a pill bottle on the bedside table and picked it up. According to the label, the bottle contained Xanax, prescribed to someone whose name I didn't recognise.

"Where did you get these?" I asked.

"I found them in a house during one of our supply runs."

"And you've been taking them?"

She nodded slightly. "Yeah. I thought they'd help me forget for a while."

"And do they?"

"They make me tired."

"You probably shouldn't be taking them."

She rolled over and snatched the bottle from me. "Don't even think about throwing them away." Rolling back to face the wall, she clutched the pills to her chest.

"I wasn't going to throw them away. I was just saying you probably shouldn't be taking someone else's prescribed drugs. Those things can be pretty powerful and they're probably addictive."

She shrugged. "If I need more, I'll get more."

"Lucy, you need to think about what you're doing."

"Leave me alone, Alex."

"Don't you want to know what we found in that Land Rover?" I asked, trying to change the subject.

"No, I don't care."

"You will when I tell you what it was. You won't believe it, actually."

"I said I don't care!" she said, turning to glare at me. "I also told you to leave me alone."

"Okay, okay, I'm going." I got up off the bed and left the room, shutting the door behind me. As I ascended the stairs to the living area, I pondered the situation. I'd known something was bothering Lucy but I hadn't realised she'd been taking pills. How long had this been going on?

The last supply run she'd taken part in had been two weeks ago so she must have had the pills at least that long.

I didn't even know if the bottle I'd seen was the only one in her possession.

I went out onto the aft deck where the footlocker was waiting. After bringing it into the living area—where Pat Benatar's *Love is a Battlefield* was coming through the speakers—I placed it on the dining table and stared at it. Hopefully, it would provide me with some answers.

In the distance, I heard the Zodiac's engine buzzing as it approached.

I looked through the window and saw Tanya and Sam making their way to the *Lucky Escape*.

Going out onto the aft deck again, I waved to them and shouted, "We should probably get out of here. Those soldiers didn't find us but by now they probably have the entire base out searching this area. It's only a matter of time before someone sees us anchored out here."

Sam gave me a thumbs up and they took the Zodiac around to the *Escape*'s stern.

I went up to the bridge and used a pair of binoculars to scan the shore. I found it hard to believe Camp Victor would only send a handful of vehicles to retrieve something as valuable as Patient Zero. Surely this entire area would be scoured by the military soon.

I couldn't see anything through the binoculars, though, so it looked like we were going to make a clean getaway.

The radio crackled and Sam's voice came through the static. "*Hey, man, let's go.*"

"Copy that," I said. I raised the anchor, started the engine, and turned the wheel so we'd be heading out into deeper water. From there, we could head south and get out of this area before we stopped again and tried to find the location of Bunker 53 in the footlocker. Sergeant Locke had said there was a map, so that should make things easier.

The Big Easy glided out into deeper water and the *Lucky Escape* sailed alongside her.

After five minutes or so, when the shoreline was far behind us, Sam's voice came from the radio again. "Look behind us, man. We got out of there just in time."

I turned around in my chair and squinted as I surveyed the shore. Unable to see anything with the naked eye, I used the binoculars and immediately saw what Sam meant.

The harbour was crawling with soldiers and military vehicles. Some of the soldiers were on the jetty, inspecting the Volvo. As I swept the binoculars over the beach, I thought I saw a familiar figure standing by a Jeep near the water's edge. Adjusting the wheel on the binoculars, I brought the man's face into focus.

When I saw the neat, close-cropped grey hair and well-tended moustache, I recognised the man immediately. Brigadier James Gordon. We'd crossed paths before. As far as I was concerned, the man was dangerous.

And right now, he was standing stock still on the beach with his hands behind his back, looking out to sea.

Staring directly at our boats.

8

"It was Brigadier Gordon," I told the others as we sat around the *Big Easy*'s dining table later that evening. Night was falling rapidly and the view of the waves beyond the waves was darkening. We'd had a dinner that consisted of pasta and meatballs and now we were talking about our next move.

Lucy had finally emerged from the cabin to eat and had chatted airily for a while but now that we were discussing the matter at hand—Vess's body and how to get it to Bunker 53—she seemed to have lost interest in our conversation.

She moved away from the table and sat in the easy chair some distance away, listening to Survivor Radio, which was still coming through the speakers.

"I bet he's the fucker who dug up Vess," Sam said. "It has to be him."

"Probably," I agreed. "The thing is, I'm sure he knows we're out here on the water. He was watching the boats as we sailed away from the harbour."

"You sure?" Sam asked.

I remembered Gordon's face as he stood on the beach, his beady eyes staring in our direction. "Yeah, pretty sure."

"Great," Lucy murmured from the chair.

"What's that supposed to mean?" I asked, turning to face her.

"It means that thanks to your little excursion onto the mainland, we're not even safe in the boats anymore. They've probably got boats of their own and they're probably out looking for us right now."

"The sea is a big place," Tanya said. "They won't find us out here. It'd be looking for a needle in a haystack. Especially now that it's getting dark and the navigation lights are switched off."

"They'll find us," Lucy said with a certainty that unnerved me.

"So let's not hang around for too long, man," Sam said, taking a handful of papers from the footlocker that now sat on the floor by the table. "Let's find out where Bunker 53 is and head in that direction." He distributed papers among himself, Tanya, and me. He offered some to Lucy but she ignored him so he threw them into a pile in the middle of the table.

I looked through the papers in front of me. There was a manila folder containing scientific jargon and chemical equations that meant absolutely nothing to me. From what I could ascertain, this was a report about Patient Zero's blood.

Putting it aside, I checked the other papers on the table and then rummaged through the remaining contents of the footlocker.

"What are you looking for?" Sam asked.

"A map. Sergeant Locke said there's a map that shows the bunker's location. I don't see it here."

"Are you sure he said there's a map?"

"Yeah, I told him I didn't know where the bunker was and he said there's a map in the vehicle." As I spoke the last three words of that sentence, a realisation hit me. "Shit. He didn't say the map was in this footlocker. He said the map was in the vehicle. This is the stuff Echo Six stole from the military base. There won't be a map here. It must be in the front of the Land Rover."

Tanya let her head drop into her hands. "We can't go back there; the area will be crawling with soldiers."

"Yeah, man," Sam said. "And the guys who took Vess and the footlocker out of the Land Rover probably took the map too."

I shook my head. "No, they didn't. We killed those guys at the crossroads and took their vehicles. They didn't have a map. They just took back the items that had been stolen from Camp Victor, which was what they'd been tasked to do. The map is still in Echo Six's Land Rover."

Sam frowned. "Dude, I agree with Tanya; that area is too hot. You saw how many soldiers there were at the harbour."

Tanya and Sam were right; there was no way we could go back to Echo Six's Land Rover now. It was simply too dangerous.

"So that's that," Lucy said. "Your plan to save the world has fallen at the first hurdle. Going ashore was a complete waste of time."

I wasn't ready to accept that just yet. Yes, this was a setback but there had to be a way forward. I just couldn't figure out what that way was right now.

"Maybe I'll sleep on it," I said.

"Sounds like a good idea, man," Sam said. "I'm beat." He got up and stretched, cracking his back. "You coming, Tanya?"

"Yeah." She got up and looked at Lucy and me. "Maybe things will look better in the morning."

"I hope so," I said.

They went out to the aft deck to take the Zodiac back to the *Lucky Escape*.

"I don't envy them," I told Lucy. "Having to sleep on the *Escape* with Marcus Vess in the storeroom isn't a pleasant prospect."

"Maybe they should sleep here," she suggested.

That wasn't such a bad idea. "Hey, guys," I said, going out onto the aft deck after them. "You can stay here if you like. For the night, I mean. We have a spare cabin." I realised that I wasn't exactly sure about Sam and Tanya's relationship. Did they even sleep together or were they just friends? I'd never asked and they'd never offered to enlighten me regarding their situation.

"Why would we want to do that?" Tanya asked.

I shrugged. "You know, with Patient Zero being on your boat and all. I just thought it might creep you out. It'd creep me out for sure. And we could all do with a good night's rest. That might be easier to achieve on a zombie-free boat."

Sam grinned. "Sounds good to me, man."

Tanya nodded. "Sure, why not?"

They came back into the living area and I closed the door against the night.

Lucy was nowhere to be seen. I assumed she'd gone to bed.

Noticing her absence, Sam said, "Is Lucy okay with this? With us staying over, I mean."

"Yeah, it was her idea."

"Okay, cool. See you in the morning then, man."

"Goodnight, Alex," Tanya said.

I gave them a little wave as they went through the door that led to the cabins belowdecks. "Goodnight."

Before I went down myself, I cleared up the dishes and cutlery and threw them in the sink so they could soak overnight. Then I turned off the radio and made sure all the windows were closed and the doors locked.

"Batten down the hatches," I murmured to myself in a pirate's voice.

Satisfied that everything was secure, I went downstairs to the cabin Lucy and I shared. When I got there, I found the door closed and locked.

"Lucy?" I said, tapping lightly on the door. "Are you going to let me in?"

There was no answer.

"Lucy?"

Still nothing. If she'd taken more Xanax, she was probably out of it by now. I couldn't sleep in the spare cabin because Sam and Tanya were in there so I went to the storeroom, grabbed a blanket, and took it upstairs to the living area.

After making myself as comfortable as I could in the easy chair and pulling the blanket up to my chin, I closed my eyes and tried to fall asleep.

My dreams were inhabited by shambling zombies and soldiers whose chests exploded into clouds of red mist. And every now and then, a recurring image would flash into my head; the memory of Brigadier James Gordon standing on a beach watching our boats sail out to sea.

9

I woke up the following morning to find an insidious mist creeping over the sea and the boats. I sat up and rubbed my eyes before checking the time on my watch. It wasn't even six o' clock yet but my uncomfortable night in the chair had ensured I'd be an early riser today.

Climbing out of the chair stiffly, I stretched. The joints in my knees and elbows cracked audibly. I staggered into the kitchen area and filled the coffee machine. Although the day had barely started, I already knew I was going to need a large dose of caffeine to face it.

While I waited for the machine to do its thing, I stared out through the windows at the misty sea. The weather conditions had reduced visibility to no more than fifty feet and I could barely see the *Lucky Escape* through the mist.

At least this would help to conceal us from the military; it would be hard to find us while the boats were hidden by a misty shroud. I had no doubt the mist would burn off later today but by then, we'd be far away from here.

But where would we go? No matter how many times I tried to solve the problem of finding Bunker 53, the only answer I came up with was to get the map from Echo Six's Land Rover.

And that was out of the question while Brigadier Gordon's men were combing the area. Besides, now the soldiers were out in force, they'd probably taken Echo Six's Land Rover back to Camp Victor. I doubted they'd leave a military vehicle in the road.

The four of us were hardly going to be able to break into a military base and get out alive.

That meant our chances of finding Bunker 53 were less than zero. The location of a secret government bunker wasn't something you could just look up online or find on a regular map.

The inability to find Bunker 53 presented us with another problem; we couldn't hold onto Marcus Vess's body indefinitely. If the virus was bringing him back to life, then eventually he was going to wake up. I didn't want to be anywhere near him when that happened.

When the coffee had finally filled the pot, I

poured some into a mug and took it out onto the foredeck. The morning was cold and I shivered slightly. The sea was relatively calm and I could hear small waves slapping rhythmically against the hull.

I leaned on the railing and sipped the hot coffee, watching the *Lucky Escape* as I did so. On board that boat was the most fearsome creature I'd ever faced, a true nightmare in the flesh. Considering the fact that we had no idea what the virus was doing to Vess's body, it might be a good idea if Sam and Tanya remained on the *Big Easy* for a while.

I had little faith that the metal crate and a locked storeroom door would hold him if he came back to life.

I heard movement behind me and turned to see Sam coming out on deck. He'd helped himself to a mug of coffee and took a swig before waving to me. "Hey, Alex. Couldn't sleep? It's hella early."

"I could ask you the same thing."

"I always get up at the asscrack of dawn, dude, so I can workout."

"You workout?"

He looked at me dubiously. "Hell, yeah! How do you think I look so ripped, man?"

I shrugged. "I thought it was due to having little food and spending a lot of time running from danger." That was how I'd lost weight. I'd just assumed Sam—who'd always been in good shape—had maintained his toned physique the same way. I didn't realised he was working at it.

He scoffed. "Once a gym rat, always a gym rat, buddy. I can't go to a gym anymore, obviously, but I still do some bodyweight exercises. Gotta keep everything tight, know what I mean?" He patted his flat stomach through his T-shirt.

One look at my physique should have told him I didn't know what he meant at all. I hadn't worked out a day in my life, unless walking to the Chinese takeaway counted as exercise.

I was going to tell this to Sam but he held up a hand, shushing me. He seemed to be listening for something.

"What's up?" I asked.

"Do you hear that?" he whispered.

I listened to the environment around us. I could hear the waves hitting the boat and seagulls in the distance but nothing out of the ordinary.

Then I heard it. Voices in the distance and the low hum of a boat engine.

"I think it's those soldiers, man," Sam said. "They're looking for us."

Because of the mist, I had no idea how far away—or how close—the other boat was. I knew that sound travelled well over the water, which could mean it was miles away. But it could just as easily be a hundred feet away, hidden by the mist.

"We need to get out of here," I said.

Sam nodded. "I'll get Tanya and we'll get the *Escape* started. He downed his coffee and left the deck.

I followed him inside but instead of going down to the cabin area, I walked through the living area and went out through the rear door to the aft deck. Once there, I climbed the ladder to the bridge and sat in the pilot's chair.

After a minute or so, Sam appeared on the aft deck with a tired-looking Tanya and gave me the thumbs up before they descended the aft ladder to the Zodiac. Instead of using the Zodiac's motor, they grabbed the paddles and rowed across to the *Escape*, obviously trying to make as little noise as possible.

I switched on the radio and dialled through the channels to see if I could pick up any sort of transmission from the unknown boat.

I couldn't pick up any chatter so I returned the radio to its original channel.

It crackled and Sam's voice said, "Okay, dude, let's get the hell out of here. I think they're south of us so we're going to head north."

"Copy that." I started the *Big Easy*'s engine, inwardly flinching as it roared to life. If the other boat was close enough that we could hear the voices of those on board, then they were sure to hear the Easy's engine.

Through the mist, I saw the Escape begin to move slowly away and I followed her, keeping a steady pace.

I searched the radio channels again and now I did pick up something.

"Foxtrot Two, do you hear that? Over."

"Sierra One, this is Foxtrot Two. I hear engines. Sounds like they're north of our position. Heading that way now. Over."

"Copy, Foxtrot Two."

Yeah, they were military all right and they were definitely looking for us. If not for this mist, they'd probably have found us already. Our only hope now was to slip away unseen. That wasn't going to be easy when we were piloting forty-two foot boats with powerful engines.

I came up alongside the *Lucky Escape* and we sailed together through the mist. Tanya was at the wheel of the Escape and she waved at me through the window. Sam was standing on the aft deck, peering at the mist in our wake.

I wondered if Lucy was still asleep. I should probably have awoken her and told her the trouble we were in but that would only have made her mood worse. She was probably in a deep sleep, anyway; a sleep aided by the pills she seemed to be taking on a regular basis.

I guessed I couldn't blame her if she wanted to run away from everything. Hell, we all did. Since the world had turned upside down, there was nothing I wanted more than to curl into a ball and block it all out. But I knew that if I did that, I wouldn't last long. In this new zombie-infested world survival was a hard-fought game that had no grand prize other than one more day of staying alive.

I heard the door below open and Lucy came out onto the aft deck. I opened the bridge door and looked down at her. "Hey, how are you doing?"

"Okay," she said, rubbing her bleary eyes. "What's going on?"

"We heard another boat in the area so we're getting out of here."

"Gordon's men?"

"Probably."

"Are they following us?"

"Yeah, I think so."

"Anything you want me to do?"

"Just sit tight for now. Hopefully we can lose them in this mist."

She nodded slowly and went back inside.

The radio crackled and I heard something that made my blood run cold.

"Delta One, this is Foxtrot Two requesting air support. Over."

"Foxtrot two, this is Delta One. Air support confirmed. ETA six minutes."

10

I wanted to shout across to Tanya to see if she'd heard the message on the radio but I didn't dare make a noise that would give away our position. When I looked through my window at the bridge of the Escape, I was in no doubt that Tanya had heard the message from Delta One. She'd paled and she looked across at me with worried eyes.

If the military was sending planes this way, we had no hope of escape. There was nowhere to run and nowhere to hide.

Tanya turned the wheel and steered the *Escape* towards the shore. As the boat peeled away, I looked at her through the bridge window with a questioning shrug.

She keyed her radio and simply said, "Follow me."

I had no reason to do otherwise so I spun the

wheel and followed. I guessed that Tanya's plan was to get to land. When the air support arrived, we were sitting ducks out here but if we could get to land, we had a chance to evade capture.

Also, if we headed into the shallows, we might get away from the boats that were following us. They probably thought we were headed out into deeper water so going in the opposite direction might fool them.

It wasn't much of a plan but it was all we had.

Lucy appeared at the foot of the ladder. "Alex, where are we going?"

"It might be a good idea to get ready to abandon ship," I told her. "We could be going ashore."

"What? Why?"

"There are planes heading our way. Or helicopters. Or something. We'll never get away as long as we're out here."

I expected her to react violently, to blow up and let out a string of curses. She didn't. Instead, she calmly said, "I'll get the weapons," and disappeared inside. In some way, that was worse than if she'd had an outburst.

We'd been sailing toward the shore for a couple of minutes at a fair pace when something huge and dark loomed out of the mist.

I cut our speed when I realised it was a rock and we were heading straight for it. Tanya had also seen it and had manoeuvred the *Lucky Escape* around the seaward side of the obstruction. I turned the wheel so that the *Big Easy* sailed past the side of the rock closer to shore.

I heard a thump and felt a shudder as the boat's hull hit something and realised I'd made the wrong choice. I'd avoided the large rock but in doing so, I'd taken the *Easy* into shallow water and we were now hitting submerged rocks.

If I turned back towards deeper water, I'd hit the rock that jutted above the water. If I turned the wheel in the opposite direction, I'd be going into even shallower water. I had no option other than to stay on course until we got past the large rock and then head for deeper water.

But that wasn't going to work either. I heard and felt another rock hit the hull and then the Easy stopped in her tracks.

We were grounded.

The bridge door opened and Lucy stuck her head inside. "Alex, what the fuck?"

"We're stuck," I said, killing the engine.

"No," she said, shaking her head. "We can't be."

"It's time to abandon ship," I told her. "We're in shallow water so we can't be far from the shore. We'll swim for land and Tanya can pick us up farther along the shore where there aren't any rocks."

Lucy was still shaking her head. "No, it isn't

going to be that easy." She pointed towards the shore.

I looked through my window and felt my heart sink.

The mist had lifted enough that visibility was improving. We were no more than a hundred feet from shore. The beach was sandy and would have been a perfect holiday destination if the world hadn't gone to hell.

Right now, the entire area was full of zombies.

Most of them shambled over the sand aimlessly, unaware of our presence. A group of five stood at the water's edge staring at us, alerted to our location by the sound of our voices.

Swimming ashore wasn't an option.

"What are we going to do?" Lucy asked.

I appraised our situation and didn't like it at all. The boat was stuck. We were stuck. And military aircraft were coming this way. I could already hear a low buzzing somewhere overhead.

Lucy heard it too. She looked up at the sky. "Sounds like a drone."

That made sense. The coast was being constantly patrolled by drones so all Delta One had to do was request that the closest aircraft be diverted to our position.

"Those things have Hellfire missiles," Lucy said. "They're going to blow us out of the water."

I shook my head vehemently. "No, they're not.

They can't. For all they know, we have Vess's body on board. They can't risk blowing it to pieces."

"I wouldn't be so sure about that," Lucy said as we heard a whistling noise that got louder in pitch with each passing second. She slid down the ladder and I followed. Zombies or not, if there was a missile heading towards us, we had to swim for shore.

The sea in front of the *Big Easy* erupted. A plume of sea water geysered into the air and rained down on the boat.

Lucy passed me a baseball bat and she grabbed a tyre iron.

"We can't leave the papers behind," I told her, running into the living area.

"Alex, come on!" she shouted at me. "That was just a warning shot. The next one will kill us!"

She was probably right. My reasoning that the military wouldn't risk blowing Vess up seemed to be misguided.

A second missile struck the area in front of the boat. This one was closer and the foredeck ripped apart in the explosion. Flames and black smoke began to rise from the bow. Maybe I'd been right about them not wanting to blow us up after all. They were trying to cripple us to make sure we couldn't escape. They didn't realise we were already grounded.

"Leave the damn papers!" Lucy shouted at me.

I couldn't let Gordon and his men get this stuff back. I just couldn't. I stuffed everything back into the footlocker and carried it out onto the aft deck. I was sure it would float when I jumped overboard.

"Oh my God, oh my God!" Lucy was looking towards the shore with panic in her eyes.

I followed her gaze and my breath caught in my throat.

The zombies, attracted by the sound of the explosion, were all coming this way now. And they weren't stopping at the water's edge. They were wading into the sea, intent on reaching us.

The *Big Easy* listed slightly onto her side and I felt cold water rush over my feet. The rocks we'd hit must have punctured the hull. The bow of the boat was on fire, the stern was sinking, and the zombies were wading towards us with a hungry hate in their yellow eyes.

11

We stood on the sinking deck with our weapons ready. The bat felt heavy in my hands. The footlocker sat on the deck behind me. Lucy stood next to me, wielding the tyre iron. I wasn't sure if we should stay on the boat and fight or get the hell out of here. If we stayed, we were in danger of being blown up by the next missile that came our way. If we swam for it, we'd swim right into the zombie horde.

Some of the creatures had almost reached the boat already. I hefted the bat and took a swing at a rotting man who was wearing a life vest. I had no idea how he'd got here or why he was wearing the vest but those things were irrelevant now. They were part of his old life. Now, he had become a creature that acted in accordance with the virus coursing through its body.

What had once been a man with hopes and dreams was now nothing more than something I had to exterminate.

The bat connected with his skull, which collapsed like an overripe watermelon. The creature collapsed into the water.

Lucy attacked a bald-headed zombie similarly dressed in a life vest. Perhaps he'd once been a friend of the man who'd become the creature that now floated in front of me. Or perhaps they'd never known each other and had simply ended up on this beach by chance. Either way, they both met the same fate as Lucy's tyre iron cleaved the bald skull in two and the creature dropped like a bag of cement into the sea.

The life vests ensured the two corpses remained afloat as other creatures waded past them to get to us.

"Why are they in the water?" Lucy asked. "They usually avoid it."

"I don't know," I admitted. I'd try to figure out their unusual behaviour later; right now, we needed an escape plan.

"We can't swim for shore," I told Lucy, "but we can swim for that big rock out there."

"Won't they follow us?"

"I hope not," I said, throwing the footlocker over the side. These zombies were ignoring their usual instinct to avoid water but could they actually swim? From what I'd seen so far, the animated corpses only had rudimentary movement. Could they perform a physical task as complex as swimming?

I doubted it. Even hybrids—which were way more capable than the shamblers we had wading towards us—couldn't swim. I'd seen a group of them fall into the sea and simply drown.

I vaulted over the railing and into the water, followed closely by Lucy. Now we had the boat between us and the creatures. I grabbed the footlocker—which was floating—and swam for the rock that jutted from the water.

I didn't look back until I scrambled out of the water, dragging the footlocker up onto the rock. The *Big Easy* was swarming with zombies now. The boat's bow was underwater and the creatures scrambled aboard easily.

They seemed to know Lucy and I were on the rock and some of them stepped off the boat into the deeper water but they flailed helplessly once they were out of their depth. They didn't exactly sink but they were unable to achieve any forward movement. They struggled and splashed as if they were drowning but they didn't actually drown.

I heard a buzzing sound that I thought was

the drone overhead but soon realised was coming from the deeper water. I looked in the direction and saw Sam and Tanya in the Zodiac, speeding towards our position. They were armed with M16s and they looked like they meant business.

Sam steered the craft so that it came up alongside the rock and Lucy and I got in. As soon as we were sitting down, he revved the engine and we sped away towards the *Lucky Escape*.

"You're such a geek, Alex," he said, motioning to the footlocker with his head. "Even in a crisis, you have to save the paperwork."

"There could be something really important in here," I told him. "I couldn't let it sink. There might be something in here that Brigadier Gordon needs to complete Operation Dead Ground. By keeping it from him, we may have saved a lot of lives."

He shrugged and looked at me incredulously. "Dude, we don't even know what Operation Dead ground is."

"We know it's not good. The clue is in the name, remember?"

He grinned and nodded.

"It might not be safe to get on board the Escape," I said. "You saw what they did to the Easy." I looked back at the burning, broken craft that had been our home and safe haven for all this time. Without that boat, I'd have been long dead. I remembered time spent on the boat with Mike and Elena. Now, like my two friends, the *Big Easy* was gone. Another casualty of the world we now inhabited; a world where nothing good can ever last.

"They won't hit the *Lucky Escape* with any missiles," Tanya said.

I frowned at her. "How can you be so sure?"

"They won't risk blowing Patient Zero up."

"For all they know, Vess might be on the Easy," I said.

She shook her head. "No, they know he's on the Escape. Before we came to rescue you, we dragged the crate up onto the deck so they could see it from the air. They can't blow up the boat because then they'd lose their precious science experiment."

Putting Vess's crate on display was good thinking but it probably meant the boats we'd heard earlier were racing towards the Escape now, hoping to board her and take the prize.

It was still too misty to see the military boats but I had no doubt they were close.

"So what's the plan?" I asked. "We can't outrun the army forever and we can't hide as long as they have air support."

"You're the brains of the group," Sam said. "Planning is your department, dude."

"I'll think of something," I said, not feeling anywhere near as confident as I sounded.

We reached the Escape and climbed quickly on board. Tanya climbed up to the bridge and got us moving. I could hear the drone but when I searched the sky for it, I couldn't see it.

I was sure it had a visual on us, though.

Cold and wet, I stood at the railing and peered into the mist in our wake. Unless my eyes were playing tricks on me, there was a dark shape back there, almost completely hidden by the mist.

"They're getting closer," I said to Sam and Lucy, pointing at the shape. "That's their boat."

Sam looked at me and for the first time in ages, his usual bravado was gone. "So what's the plan?"

As I'd already told everyone, we couldn't run forever and the drone gave Gordon's men a bird's eye view at all times so we couldn't hide. Not in the boat, anyway.

"The only way to hide from the drone is to enter a building," I said.

Sam gestured around us. "Dude, there aren't any buildings out here. We're in the sea."

Ignoring the fact that he was stating the obvious, I said, "How quickly can we hotwire a car, load Vess on board, and drive away?"

He thought about it for a moment and then

shrugged. "I don't know. A couple of minutes maybe."

"We have to get to land," I said. "Out here, we have no chance. If we can quickly get into a car and drive to a town, we can hide out in the buildings. Maybe even use the sewers. That's the only way we can avoid the army's airborne eyes."

"You're forgetting one thing," Lucy said. "Zombies. If we go to any town, it's going to be crawling with zombies."

I nodded. She was right but what choice did we have? "We either risk it or end up being captured by the military."

"Not much of a choice, Dude." Sam turned towards the shore. "If we study the map, we should find a good place to land. There's bound to be a harbour somewhere around here. I'll check it out." He went up to the bridge to talk to Tanya.

"You okay?" I asked Lucy.

She looked at me with eyes that betrayed no emotion. "Well, our boat's totalled and we're on the run from the army, so no, I'm not okay."

"Sorry, I was only asking."

"And what did you expect me to say? That I'm fine with all this? If you'd listened to me and not gone ashore to answer that radio call, we'd be happily sailing around without a care in the world right now."

"No," I said, shaking my head. "We wouldn't. You grabbed those pills weeks ago so you hardly had no care in the world. You were already depressed. And I get it. This situation we're in—"

"Shut up about the fucking pills, Alex. They help me, okay? Is that so fucking bad?"

"No, of course not. It's just that—"

"So we're agreed. Now leave the pills out of it. What I choose to do is none of your damned business."

I held up my hands, telling I wasn't going to interfere anymore. She was right that it was none of my business what she did to handle her emotions, although I'd thought our relationship meant we would probably talk about such things before resorting to drugs.

My biggest fear was that taking the pills meant Lucy didn't have her head in the game and she might endanger herself or others. In this new world, survival meant having your head on a swivel and staying alert. The pills Lucy had been taking were dulling her edge.

Sam came back down the ladder. "Guys, there's a small harbour a couple of miles ahead. We can't all fit in the Zodiac with Vess so Tanya is going to take the Escape right up to the jetty. You guys get Vess off the boat while Tanya and I grab a car. Simple."

I hoped it was going to be as easy as Sam thought.

"What about a nearby town?" I asked.

He nodded. "There's a seaside town called Frinton-on-Sea."

"Sounds ideal." Being a seaside town, Frinton would have hotels and shops close to the beach. We could be undercover quite quickly.

"Let's lock and load," Sam said, going inside to get the weapons.

Unfortunately, we'd lost the guns that were on board the *Big Easy*, which meant we now had two M16s, and two Walther PPKs between us. And the ammo for these guns was running dangerously low. Each M16 had a spare magazine but the Walthers had only the bullets that were already loaded.

"Let's hope we don't run into too many zombies," Sam said, examining the remaining ammunition.

That was a hope I definitely shared. We'd seen a few towns during our travels and all of them had been swarming with undead creatures. The army was rounding up people for the survivors camps from villages and isolated communities but they seemed to be leaving larger towns alone. It was probably too dangerous to mount a rescue mission in an area where thousands of zombies roamed the streets.

I had no idea what the population of Frinton-on-Sea was but there was no doubt in my mind that most of the people who lived there were now infected.

The bridge door opened and Tanya shouted down to us. "The harbour is dead ahead."

I wished she'd used different words.

12

The *Lucky Escape* glided into the harbour and Sam jumped off. After hastily tying the mooring rope, he sprinted away in search of a vehicle. Lucy and I grabbed an end each of Vess's crate and heaved it off the boat and onto the cement jetty. Tanya followed us, carrying the footlocker.

We'd distributed the weapons so that Tanya and Sam had the M16s and Lucy and I had the handguns. I also had my baseball bat slung over my shoulder. We weren't exactly equipped to take on a large number of enemies—be they soldiers or zombies—but this was an escape mission and we'd agreed that if we got into trouble, we'd run rather than fight.

"Come on," Tanya said, heading along the jetty. "That boat won't be far behind us."

We made our way to the end to land, where

Sam had already hotwired an RV and was waiting for us with the engine running.

He climbed out and helped us load Patient Zero into the vehicle. He was grinning the entire time, obviously pleased with himself. "Good thinking on my part, huh? Something large enough to carry us all."

"Also easier for the drone to spot," I said. I didn't mean it maliciously but I also thought that this wasn't the time for self-congratulation. We were still in danger and until we'd found somewhere safe, I couldn't relax.

Sam looked crestfallen but he perked himself up and said, "We're not going far in it, man. The town is just there." He pointed at Frinton-on-Sea, which was no more than a couple of miles away.

"Okay," I said. "Let's go." I climbed into the back of the RV with Lucy while Sam got behind the wheel and Tanya took the passenger seat. We rumbled away from the harbour and I looked seaward. The military vessel, which looked more like a civilian boat the army had commandeered, was landing at the harbour.

"Don't worry," Sam said, putting his foot down. "We'll be long gone before they find a vehicle. I slashed the tyres of all the other cars in the car park."

"Good thinking," I said, in part because I felt a little guilty about my earlier jab at him but also because it was a smart thing he'd done. We might actually have a chance of escape.

Tanya turned around in her seat and asked, "What exactly is the plan, Alex? If we hole up in a building, they'll find us eventually."

"We're not going to hole up," I told her. "The drone will probably watch us enter a building but then it will lose visual. We'll slip into the next building, and then the next, until it loses us. If we can get into the sewers, we should be able to get far enough away that we can get back to street level and find another vehicle while the army is still searching for us in the wrong area."

"Sounds great except for the zombies," Sam said. "There's bound to be a shitload of them in town."

"We'll just have to deal with them as we encounter them," I told him. "I can't account for everything and I never said this would be easy."

He nodded. "Fair enough, man."

We reached the outskirts of Frinton a few minutes later. Sam slammed on the brakes and the RV juddered to a stop.

"What's wrong?" I asked, looking between the front seats at the sight beyond the windscreen. When I saw what was there, it was obvious that my question was moot.

The streets of Frinton were full of shambling zombies. I'd feared that the town would be full of the creatures and unfortunately I'd been correct. There must be at least a thousand undead monsters roaming the streets.

"What now?" Sam asked.

"Get us out of here," I said. "We'll have to find another town."

But before Sam could put the RV into reverse, an explosion rocked the vehicle. My ears rang from the sound. Rocks and bricks rained down on top of the RV, clanging off the metal roof.

"Fuck!" Sam said. "There's no road behind us anymore. They blew the fucker up!"

"They're trying to trap us," I said.

The zombies ahead of us began to turn in our direction and shamble towards us. We couldn't stay in the vehicle; we'd be surrounded by a thousand zombies in less than a minute.

I looked desperately through the windows for a place to go. The only option was a five-storey block of flats. "Let's get inside there," I said.

No one argued or questioned that decision. We couldn't go backwards, we couldn't go forwards, and we couldn't stay where we were. We unloaded the crate and footlocker and carried them to the flats.

When we got to the main door, my heart sank. It had been smashed and pulled off its hinges. The zombies would be able to follow us inside.

"This isn't good, man," Sam said as he stepped over broken glass and into the building.

There was a ground floor flat here but its door had also been smashed open.

A set of cement steps led up to the next level.

I looked back at the RV. A dozen zombies had already reached it and were clawing at the vehicle as if they thought we were still inside. The rest of the horde had seen us enter the block of flats and were coming this way.

I prayed that we'd find a flat on one of the upper floors with an intact door. If we didn't, then we were finished.

Sam took the lead, M16 braced against his shoulder, and Tanya took the rear—M16 in one hand, footlocker in the other— while Lucy and I manhandled the crate up the steps.

We reached the first floor to find the doors similarly broken.

"The place has been looted," Sam said.

"We'll keep going up," I said. "If we can't find a flat with an intact door, we'll have to barricade ourselves inside a bedroom or something. Any room that has a door we can defend."

Sam sighed and ascended the stairs to the next level. When the rest of us arrived, he'd already gone up to the level after that because every flat door down here was smashed.

"We're going to die in here," Lucy said calmly and with a certainty that unnerved me.

"No, we're not," I assured her, although I knew I was probably lying. I could hear the zombies on the steps below us.

There was no way down.

13

As we reached the fourth floor and found more broken doors, Sam came down the steps and said, “Come on, we can get onto the roof. That door is the only one that isn’t fucked up.”

I wasn’t sure how great a plan going out onto the roof was. The drone would have no problem spotting us up there. But what other choice did we have? At least we could close the door on the zombies that were shuffling up the steps below us.

What we’d do after that, I had no idea but anything was better than being ripped apart by the undead on these concrete steps.

Sam helped us with the crate and we managed to get through the door and out onto the flat roof. Sam closed the door behind us.

We put the crate down on the gravelled roof and Tanya put the footlocker next to it. "Now what?" she asked.

I went to the roof's edge and looked down, immediately wishing I hadn't. The building was totally surrounded with zombies and from here, I realised that my estimate of a thousand undead was inadequate. There must have been at least three thousand zombies roaming around down there.

They'd left the RV alone and now they were all focused on the flats but there were so many of them that they couldn't all fit in the building so some of them wandered aimlessly around while others got stuck in tight clusters.

I raised my head and looked for the drone. There was no cover up here. As soon as the aircraft flew overhead, it would spot us easily.

A loud bang sounded on the door. Through a small glass window in the door, I saw a rotting face appear. It was joined by another and then another. The banging continued.

"Can they break through?" Tanya asked.

I didn't answer her. I was thinking about the force that many bodies would exert on the wood until eventually the hinges gave way. What the hell would we do when that happened?

I heard the drone somewhere in the distance.

Shielding my eyes from the sun, I searched the skies until I saw the black shape coming this way. Once the drone got a visual on us, Gordon would send his men to deal with the zombies and take us off the roof.

They'd have a problem dealing with the horde, though, which meant that by the time they got to us, we might be already dead if that door gave way.

"What do we do?" Tanya asked. "What's our exit strategy?"

"We don't have one," I admitted. "We're stuck here."

"That isn't what I wanted to hear, Alex."

"I know. I'm sorry,"

The drone was getting closer. I looked in its direction and wondered if shooting at it would do any good. Probably not; we'd just be prolonging the inevitable. Gordon would realise where we were anyway when he saw the number of zombies milling around this particular building.

I squinted at the black airborne shape I'd thought was the drone, realising suddenly that it was in fact a Chinook helicopter. Its twin rotors were impossible to mistake. So we were going to be captured after all, assuming the helicopter got here before the door broke. We might as well surrender. Better to be captured by the army than torn apart by undead teeth and nails.

The four of us stood together while the Chinook descended. The wind whipped up by the twin rotors scattered gravel across the roof and made it an effort to stand in the same place without being blown away.

The helicopter didn't land; it hovered at the edge of the roof and the ramp at its rear opened up. A man stepped forward. He wasn't wearing an army uniform. Instead he wore black cargo pants and a tight blue T-shirt over his heavily-muscled frame. An assault rifle was slung over his shoulder. When I saw his face and buzz cut hair, I recognised him immediately.

Ian Hart, head of security at Apocalypse Island. He was the man who'd overseen our mission when we'd worked for the government facility. I'd never been happier to see him than I was at this moment.

He gestured for us to come aboard the Chinook and said, "Come with me if you want to live."

We grabbed the crate and footlocker and took them up the ramp and into the interior of the helicopter. The rear ramp closed and I felt the floor beneath my feet move as we ascended.

"You said that exact same line the first time we met," I told Hart.

"Did I? Take a seat and we'll get the hell out of here. Looks like you've got yourselves into a spot of bother."

We sat in the seats that were attached to the walls and strapped ourselves in. The interior of the aircraft was noisy and the only way to be heard was to shout so we remained silent.

I wondered what Hart was doing here. Apocalypse Island was off the coast of Scotland, hundreds of miles north of here. How had he found us?

I wasn't about to look a gift horse in the mouth. My questions could wait.

We flew for half an hour before I felt a twinge in my stomach due to the helicopter descending. We touched down and the engines were switched off.

"Here we are," Hart said, unstrapping himself from his seat and standing by the ramp as it opened. "Site Bravo One. Before we go into the facility, I have one question. What's in those boxes?"

"The small one contains papers and documents," I told him. "The large crate has the body of Patient Zero inside. If you have a secure room, you'll want to lock the crate inside it."

He frowned, confused. "You said it was his body."

I nodded. "But I didn't say he was dead."

Hart raised a questioning eyebrow.

"The virus might be bringing him back to life," I said.

Two men armed with assault rifles and dressed similarly had appeared at the foot of the ramp. "Get this crate into one of the cells," Hart told them. "And make sure it's guarded around the clock."

I knew why he was being so cautious. When we'd been at Apocalypse Island, our friend Jax had turned and taken out a number of personnel before she'd escaped the facility.

"Follow me," he said. "I take it you've had some adventures since we last spoke."

"You can say that again, man," Sam said.

We followed Hart down the ramp and found ourselves standing on the tarmac of a small runway near two aircraft hangars. Beyond the hangars, a large three-storey building that had the unmistakable boxy look of a government facility stood in the sunshine. The morning light reflected off the building's windows, which seemed to have been treated with some sort of silver-coloured reflective material.

"Site Bravo One," Hart said, gesturing to the building. "We had to abandon Apocalypse Island in the end. Too many bloody zombies on the island. We don't have that problem here. This island is free of the bastards."

"We're on an island?" The area around the complex was covered with trees so from this vantage point, it looked like we were in the middle of a forest.

"Yes, we are," Hart said, leading us across the tarmac to the silver-windowed building. "It's not as big as Apocalypse Island and it's mostly trees apart from what you see here. There's a harbour on the west side. That road there leads to it." He pointed at a road that led into the trees. "What do you think?"

"Looks pretty cool," I said. "And the lack of zombies makes it better than the old place."

"That's a definite plus," he said. "So, I was going to ask what you lot have been up to but since you told me what's in that crate, I think the answer is obvious."

"How did you find us?" I asked him.

"We've been monitoring the military radio channels for a while now. The chatter at Camp Victor went off the charts. We knew something big was happening but had no idea what. Then we saw that you were in the area and we put two and two together."

Now I was confused. "What do you mean you saw we were in the area?"

He showed me his Ministry of Defence ID badge. "Remember when we issued you with one of these? All these badges have tracking chips installed. So when we discovered something was going down at Camp Victor, we consulted the computer to see which operatives we had in the area. And there you were. We tracked you as far as the harbour."

We reached the door to the building and he swiped his ID badge through the digital lock. "When we realised you'd left your boat, we followed the explosions and the smoke." He chuckled. "We knew we'd find you there."

"Well you didn't come a moment too soon," Tanya told him. "A few more minutes on that roof and we'd have been zombie chow."

"Glad to help," he said, leading us through a large tiled foyer and through another locked door which he opened with his badge. "Now perhaps you can help us. We've suspected for a while that something dodgy has been going on at Camp Victor but we haven't been able to collect any useable info. We're short-staffed, due to the fact that most of our employees became zombies. You know how it is. So I'd be grateful for any intelligence you might have."

"Sure," I said. "But I'd like to ask you a question first."

"Okay, shoot."

"Do you know the location of Bunker 53?"

His eyes narrowed. "Why do you ask?"

"You'll know why when we tell you how we

happen to have Patient Zero's body. Bunker 53 is a government bunker and this is a government facility so you know where the bunker is, right?"

He nodded slowly. "Yes, we know where it is."

"Great," I said.

He unlocked another door, this one opening into a large auditorium. It reminded me of the room at the Apocalypse Island facility where we'd been given our instruction to carry out Operation Wildfire.

"Take a seat," Hart said. "Marilyn will be along momentarily."

"She still in charge?" Sam asked.

Hart nodded. "She is indeed. It was Marilyn who made the decision to abandon the old island and come here. That was a tough decision to make but in the end, she saved a lot of lives. We wouldn't have lasted much longer there."

Sam, Tanya, and Lucy sat in the front row. I sat behind them. I'd never been a front row kind of guy.

The seats faced a darkened stage. After a few seconds, the stage lights came on and Marilyn MacDonald appeared. She was impeccably dressed in a dark blue skirt and white blouse. Her blonde hair was pinned up on her head and she wore her usual thick-rimmed glasses. Her job as director of this facility must have been fraught with stress but she exuded an air of calm confidence.

She looked down at us from the stage and said, “Good to see you again. Now, perhaps you can tell me how you got your hands on Patient Zero.”

14

Between us, we told her the story of what had happened since we'd received the call for help from Echo Six. MacDonald listened intently, interrupting every now and then to clarify a detail or ask us to provide more information on a particular part of our tale.

When we were finished, she nodded thoughtfully. "We need to know exactly what Locke meant when he referred to Operation Dead Ground."

"What about Bunker 53?" I asked. "That's where Locke said Vess's body should go. To Dr Sarah Ives."

"The body stays here," she said. "We don't have any scientists left to study it but now that it's secure, I don't recommend taking it anywhere else. Especially if it could come back to life at any moment."

"I agree with your reasoning," I told her. "But he was quite specific. Bunker 53 and Dr Ives. He must have said that for a reason."

She considered that for a moment before saying, "We'll bring Dr Ives here. She can examine the body in this facility. We have equipment and a lab she can use. I won't compromise the safety of my people by having the body taken out into the world. Too much can go wrong. As long as it stays within this facility, we can ensure it won't hurt anyone else."

I wasn't so sure I shared in her optimism regarding that point. The fact that they'd had to move to this new facility because the old one was overrun with zombies showed that the people here weren't exactly infallible when it came to security.

Not to mention the fact that all the scientists I'd seen on Apocalypse Island were now either dead or undead. That didn't fill me with confidence at all.

"I suggest you enjoy a meal in our cafeteria while I arrange for Dr Ives to be escorted here. Perhaps when she arrives we might find out why Sergeant Locke had specifically requested that Vess's body be sent to her."

"I'll show you to the cafeteria," Hart said. "The

food is good and I imagine you've been living on whatever you can get your hands on out there, which might be adequate but not necessarily pleasant."

Actually, we'd eaten fairly well on the boats. I certainly didn't have any complaints. But the fact that I'd lived on low-quality food before the zombie apocalypse meant that I probably wasn't the best person to judge.

When we got to the cafeteria—a busy place with a long food counter and metal tables bolted to the floor—I found the food to be no better or worse than anything else I'd eaten either before or after the apocalypse. It was standard fare, really: bacon, eggs, baked beans, and toast with a mug of hot tea.

The four of us sat at a table near the window and ate in silence. Hart had disappeared to do some chore or other and had promised to be back soon.

I finished before the others and pushed my plate away with a satisfied belch.

Tanya, who was sitting next to me, hit my arm. "Alex, don't be a pig."

"Sorry," I said, picking up my mug and drinking some of my tea. "Hey, does anyone else feel a sense of relief?"

"I'm glad they took that damned body off our hands," Tanya said.

Sam nodded. "Yeah, man, I really don't want to be around when that fucker wakes up."

Lucy didn't say anything. She just kept eating.

"We're going to need new boats," Tanya said after a short silence.

I felt a pang of loss for the *Big Easy*. She'd seen me through some bad times and good times.

"Maybe we should get bigger boats next time," Sam suggested.

A quote from Jaws came to mind but I kept it to myself.

"Why do you want something bigger?" Tanya asked. "Are you trying to prove something?"

Sam scoffed. "No, I just thought that more space would be nice."

We fell into a short silence again which was broken, surprisingly, by Lucy. "What do you think Bunker 53 is like?"

"No idea," I said.

"I think I saw something about the emergency bunkers on TV once," she said. "They had everything. Like, swimming pools and gyms and even shops. All hidden away behind doors that were impregnable. Totally secure from whatever danger there is outside."

I recalled our conversation when she'd said she wanted to feel safe and wondered if she wanted to live somewhere like Bunker 53. It was probably everything she'd been talking about.

"Yeah, I read about them somewhere," Sam said. "The government chooses a cross-section of society and tells them about the bunker. Then, when the shit hits the fan, those people go there and become the future of the human race or something. The survivors of whatever tragedy takes place. I'm pretty sure a lot of politicians get to go there too, so the future of the human race doesn't seem so great after all."

"Imagine being locked away from all this tragedy, though," Lucy said. This was the most animated I'd seen her in a long time. "Imagine knowing you were safe from all this crap."

"Booooring," Sam said.

"At least you wouldn't wake up every day wondering if it was your last," she told him.

"Dude, any of us could die on any given day and not just because there are zombies in the world. You could have a heart attack, get cancer, or fall off a cliff. Every day could be your last no matter where you are."

She looked out of the window at the aircraft hangars and ignored him.

That put a dampener on the conversation and we again fell into silence. When Hart appeared five minutes later, he was a welcome relief from the tension that had descended over the table.

"Bad news, I'm afraid," he said. "Marilyn got in

contact with Bunker 53 and they won't let Dr Ives come here."

"So what do we do now?" I asked.

Marilyn is worried about letting Vess's body off this island but she's had to concede that Ives may be able to do something important if she has access to it. As you said, Alex, Locke did specify her and he must have done so for a reason. So we're taking the body to Bunker 53."

"We?" I asked.

"I've been told to put a team together. We'll be carrying out this operation under the strictest safety measures. Any of you are welcome to join the team."

We all nodded. Sitting around in a government cafeteria wasn't really our style. even Lucy seemed eager to go, although I wondered if that was more to do with her desire to see what Bunker 53 was like than to deliver Patient Zero's body to Dr Ives.

"We'll meet in the lecture hall in half an hour and go over the plan," Hart said. "Here are your replacement badges so you can get through the doors. Just follow the signs to the hall and I'll see you there."

He placed four laminated cards onto the table. They were identical to our old ones with our names, photos—they'd used the same photos they'd taken last time—and the Ministry of

Defence symbol, a crowned wreath encircling crossed swords, a bird, and an anchor.

"Are these bugged too?" I asked.

"Of course," he said. "All of our badges have locator chips. Don't complain, Alex. If not for us picking up your location, you'd still be stuck on that roof in Frinton."

He had a point. I attached my badge to my T-shirt.

"Do we get weapons too?" Sam asked.

Hart grinned. "Of course. After the operational briefing, we'll get our gear together and head out."

Sam nodded. "Excellent."

"See you in thirty," Hart said before leaving the cafeteria.

"Working for the government again," I said as the others pinned on their badges. "This wasn't how I saw my future when I was at college."

"Don't worry about it, man," Sam said. "This is only a temporary gig, just like before. If we play our cards right, we can get some sweet weapons and some more ammo."

"I wonder what they're going to call this operation," Tanya wondered aloud.

"How about Operation Wake the Dead?" I asked.

She hit my arm again. "Don't even joke about that, Alex."

"Okay," I said, rubbing the sore spot where she'd punched me. I may have meant it as a joke but that joke hid a fearful truth. I was worried about what might happen if Vess woke up while we were transporting him to the bunker.

Marilyn MacDonald was right; Vess must never be allowed out into the world. If he woke up and we failed to stop him, anything he did, anyone he killed, would be on us.

Not that we'd be alive to know about it.

15

The name of the operation was Operation Charon. It was written on a whiteboard that had been set up in front of the stage in the auditorium. Next to the whiteboard was a large flat screen.

The name of the operation made sense. Charon was a figure in Greek mythology who ferried souls from the land of the living to the land of the dead. That was what we'd be doing; ferrying a dead soul.

I just hoped he stayed dead.

Hart stood by the board, along with a white-coated woman who introduced herself as Dr Lake. As a medical doctor, she was the closest Site Bravo One had to a scientist so she'd been given the task of reading the papers from the footlocker.

Three members of Hart's security team sat on the front row of seats. Hart introduced them as Josh Hamilton, Caroline Waters, and Andy Fletcher. They were all dressed in blue T-shirts and black cargo pants like Hart and—also like Hart—they were in good shape and looked like they meant business.

"Operation Charon," Hart said, pointing to the title on the board. "A simple transportation of cargo from this island to Bunker 53. The only difference is between this and any other run of the mill transportation operation is that this cargo might wake up en route."

In any other situation, that might have got a laugh from the audience. But this was sombre business and everyone was silent.

"We take the cargo via Chinook helicopter to this area." A map appeared on the screen that showed the coast of Western Cornwall. "Here," Hart said, pointing at a spot a few miles inland from Land's End, "is where Bunker 53 is located. Takes one hour to get there from here. Once we arrive at the bunker, we drop off the body to a Dr Sarah Ives. Then we leave and return to base. Any questions?"

Caroline Waters spoke up. "What are the safety measures in place to ensure our survival if the cargo wakes up, sir?"

"Good question," Hart said. "Vess's body is

inside a metal crate. We are going to place the crate inside a small metal cage. If Vess wakes up and gets out of the crate, he'll still have the cage to deal with. I'm not saying the cage will hold him but it should give us enough time to kill him."

"Kill him?" Josh Hamilton asked. "If we're going to kill him, then why not just do it now and save ourselves the bother of transporting him to the bunker, sir?"

"Killing Vess is a last resort," Hart said. "The blood and tissues of his body are unique. They might even hold the key to defeating this bloody virus someday. The ideal situation is that Vess ends up on an operating table surrounded by scientists who can study him and come up with something that will put an end to this situation the world finds itself in. We've fashioned vaccines before and they worked with varying degrees of effectiveness, but with access to Patient Zero, the scientists could come up with something really life-changing."

"Understood, sir," Hamilton said.

"Listen, we're not taking any chances," Hart said. "We'll have guns trained on the crate for the entire flight. If anything goes wrong we shoot to kill. Those are MacDonald's orders. We cannot let Vess escape into the world under any circumstances. Does everyone understand that?"

We all nodded.

"Before we leave, Dr Lake has a few words. Maybe this will impress upon you how important that body is."

"Thanks, Ian," Dr Lake said. She addressed the room. "I've been studying the papers that came from Camp Victor. It seems that Brigadier James Gordon—the man in charge of the camp—has been doing some experiments of his own. Well, his scientists have, anyway. But instead of using Vess's blood and tissue to formulate a vaccine or antidote, they've used it to develop a bomb."

A shocked hush fell over the room.

"A bomb?" Sam asked. "You mean a bomb to drop on the zombies, right?"

She shook her head. "No, I don't. Gordon's scientists have developed a biological weapon that delivers an airborne version of the virus. From what I can tell from the notes, any human beings that breathe the airborne toxin become savage killing machines."

"Like the hybrids," I said.

"Not quite. Those affected become like Patient Zero. He's faster than any hybrid, and more deadly. And instead of simply biting or scratching to pass on the virus, he kills instantly by tearing his victims' heads from their bodies."

I closed my eyes and remembered my friend

Johnny Drake. He'd been killed by Vess, his head and spinal cord ripped from his body.

"I don't get it," I said. "Why would they make a weapon that turns people into killing machines?"

"Gordon is a military man. He thinks in terms of power and weapons to achieve that power. I understand from checking the records that he was about to be forcibly retired by the army. He served in the Middle East some years ago and did good work there but lately he was becoming more of a nuisance to the powers that be in the military with his xenophobic attitude and increasing paranoia. When the apocalypse hit, his retirement was forgotten. The army needed every soldier they could get their hands on."

She shrugged. "It looks like Gordon used the situation to create his own private army, made up of soldiers who thought like him, and began his own private war."

"A war against whom?" I asked. "The undead?"

Dr Lake shook her head. "No. Some of the papers I've looked at were from his personal journal. He welcomes the zombie apocalypse. He believes it will weaken the enemies of Britain and that he'll be a national hero when he uses his bomb to destroy what's left of those countries. When this situation is finally over, Gordon wants Britain to be the only country left standing. And then recolonisation of the world can begin."

"That doesn't make sense," I said. "If he wants to destroy other countries, how is turning their populations into murderous zombies going to do that? Those places would become uninhabitable because of the murderous zombies."

"He's planned for that," she said. "The airborne version of the virus kills its host after five or six hours."

I nodded, understanding. Now it made sense. Set off the bomb and create killing machines. The killing machines kill everyone else and then they themselves die, meaning no one would be left alive. And then Gordon's army steps in to take over.

"So do the killing machine zombies kill the shambling zombies as well?" I wondered aloud.

"I don't know," Dr Lake said. "I don't think Gordon knows either. His scientists wanted to carry out an initial trial of the weapon but they needed to do that in a place that was contained in case anything went wrong. From the notes, it doesn't look like they've performed that trial yet."

"Thank God," Hart said. "Once we get back from Bunker 53, taking down Brigadier Gordon and Camp Victor will be our next priority."

"I have a question," Lucy said, holding up her hand.

"Of course," Hart said, "What is it?"

"What's Bunker 53 like?"

"I have absolutely no idea. As far as I know, it's a survival bunker, not a facility like this one or our old place. The people inside are just supposed to survive, nothing else. That's why they wouldn't send Dr Ives here; the people inside the bunker won't leave until the apocalypse is over. I didn't even know they had scientists there until you arrived and mentioned Ives."

"Okay," Lucy said. "Thanks."

I wondered if Lucy was going to be coming back with us from the bunker or if she was going to try and convince the authorities there to let her stay. I couldn't blame her if that was the case but I'd miss her terribly.

There was a time in my life when I'd have thought that the best way to deal with an apocalypse was to ride it out locked safely away inside a bunker. It would almost be a dream come true as long as they had plenty of food and video games.

But something inside me had changed and I no longer wanted to hide away. There was too much to do, too many people to help. How would I feel if the entire world went to hell while I sat safely inside a bunker and didn't try to help in some way, no matter how small?

I still didn't blame Lucy if that was what she

wanted to do but it wouldn't suit me at all. Not anymore.

Hart clapped his hands together once and said, "Right, if there are no more questions, let's get our weapons and get to the chopper."

16

Twenty minutes later, we were in the Chinook and heading to Bunker 53. This time we were all wearing flight helmets to block out the noise of the rotors and to enable radio communication between ourselves.

Despite the radios, no one spoke. Our attention was firmly fixed on the small metal cage, and the crate within it, that had been strapped to the floor of the helicopter. So far, the crate had been quiet but I realised that even if Vess was pounding on the inside right now, none of us would hear it due to the noise in the Chinook.

The first clue we'd have to his revival would be when he punched his way through the crate.

We were all armed with L119A1 Close Quarters Battle Carbines. This rifle was much shorter than the M16 and much more manoeuvrable in a tight space. The muzzle of every gun was pointed at the cage.

The only time I allowed my attention to wander from Vess's crate was when I glanced out through the tail ramp—which was open—at the countryside rolling past beneath us. The pilot had been instructed to fly low in case we had to discharge our weapons and that meant I could see a lot of detail as we passed over the landscape.

Most places looked abandoned. The roads were strewn with empty cars and some houses we flew over had been burned for some reason. We passed over three hordes of zombies that were concentrated in small towns. The creatures either roamed aimlessly or stood stock still in the dormant state.

The only other movement I spotted was a convoy of military vehicles driving along one of the roads. The smaller vehicles seemed to be escorting two four-ton lorries so I assumed they were taking survivors to some camp or other.

When we reached our destination and the Chinook began its descent into a quarry, I felt relieved that we hadn't had to fire our weapons in the chopper. Despite the manoeuvrability of the CQB rifles, it would have been too easy to end up caught in a crossfire from someone aiming at Vess.

The Chinook landed and we all piled out. Waters, Hamilton, and Fletcher carried the cage, to which someone had thoughtfully attached leather carrying straps. We were standing in what looked like a normal quarry. I looked around the area for some sort of door or passage that would lead to Bunker 53 but saw nothing of the sort.

Hart was similarly scanning the area with a frown on his face. "Must be here somewhere," he muttered. Taking out a slip of paper from his pocket, he consulted it and pointed at the southernmost edge of the quarry. "It's somewhere there, apparently."

We made our way to the rock wall and discovered a number of camouflage nets that had rocks and gravel applied to them to make them look like part of the quarry wall.

Pushing them aside, we came face to face with a large steel door that was at least twenty feet wide and twelve feet high.

"This is the place," Hart said. He found a small console on the door that housed a single metal button. He pressed it and we waited.

Looking closely at the area around us, I noticed a number of small cameras attached to the rocks, all pointing at us.

A male voice came from the console. "Yes?"

Hart leaned closer to the console and spoke. "Ian Hart. Site Bravo One. You spoke to my superior Marilyn MacDonald regarding the delivery of a package."

"Hold on."

There was a tense few minutes of silence during which we all trained our attention and guns on the cage. This was the worst possible place for Vess to escape. If he got out here and we didn't stop him, he'd be free to go anywhere, do anything. We should have left him in the Chinook until we knew the people in the bunker were going to let us inside.

Finally, there was a buzz and the clanking noise of disengaging locks. The door swung inward slowly, revealing a wide cement corridor that ran into the earth, sloping slightly downwards.

There was no one there to greet us. We proceeded through the door and it swung shut behind us, the heavy locks engaging again. The corridor was lit by pale yellow lights set into the ceiling.

The same male voice that had spoken to Hart through the console now came out of a tinny speaker on the wall. "Continue individually to the green line."

I noticed a green line painted on the floor twenty feet ahead of us. Beyond that was a second door identical to the one we'd just passed through.

"You first, Alex," Sam said, pushing me forward.

"Why me?" I asked.

"Don't worry, dude. If they kill you, we'll avenge your death."

"That's hardly comforting," I said. I stepped up to the green line and stopped. I noticed a couple of cameras on the walls beside me. Scanners?

"There are no weapons allowed in the bunker," the tinny voice said. "Please place your weapon in the bin to your left."

"Are you kidding?" I said. "You know what's in that crate, right?"

"The crate will be dealt with presently. Please place your weapon in the bin provided."

I turned to Hart with a questioning look on my face.

He shrugged. "I assume that as soon as they open the next door, their own security team will guard the cage. The quicker we get through this, the quicker their security will come out here."

Feeling as if I was making a terrible mistake, I placed the CQB rifle into the large plastic bin and waited.

"Step forward to the white line," the voice told me. The white line was painted just in front of the second door. I moved to it and waited while the others went through a similar process and joined me one by one.

Finally, we all stood before the second door. I found it ironic that they weren't letting us inside with weapons but they were allowing Patient Zero into their precious bunker.

The door clanked and slid open. I'd expected to see the interior of the bunker beyond but the cement corridor simply continued downward at a slight angle.

"Let's move!" Hart said. "We need to hand over the cargo ASAP."

We all took hold of the cage—four people on each side—and jogged along the corridor. We were totally unarmed now thanks to the bunker's security system and if Vess got out, we had no way to stop him.

I finally saw something ahead. Another door. But beside this one, a lighted booth was set into the wall and behind its Plexiglass window sat a large man with receding hair. He was surrounded by computer consoles that showed the view from each of the cameras in the quarry and the corridor and a microphone through which he'd been speaking to us.

"Welcome to Bunker 53," he said. "As you requested, Dr Sarah Ives will be along shortly, as well as Charles Hines, the head of our little community."

He pressed a button and the door opened. Muzak floated out through the opening, as if we were about to enter an elevator. But instead of an elevator, the door opened onto a large blue-carpeted waiting room, complete with chairs whose upholstery matched the colour of the carpet and low tables upon which sat small stacks of magazines.

It seemed like the people in this bunker were trying to pretend the world wasn't going to hell. Knowing what I knew about the world outside made the waiting room seem surreal.

A door opened and a man and woman entered. He had collar-length black hair and wore a shirt and tie. I placed him in his forties.

The woman was much younger, probably early twenties. She had shoulder-length red hair and wore glasses. She also wore a white lab coat, which was encouraging at least.

"Dr Ives?" Hart asked.

She nodded. "Yes, I'm Dr Ives. I understand you wanted to see me. Something important, I was told."

"Perhaps we could conduct this conversation somewhere else," Hart suggested. "After you get your security team to lock the package securely away." He indicated the cage on the blue-carpeted floor.

"We'll get right on that," the man said. He held out his hand to Hart. "Charles Hines. I'm in charge here."

"There's no time for pleasantries," Hart said, ignoring the proffered hand. "We need to get this locked up now."

Hines frowned. "I was told it's a dead body."

"It's dead at the moment," Hart said. "There are no guarantees it's going to stay that way."

Hines's face paled. "And you brought it here? There's been some mistake. You can't bring a...whatever that is...in here."

To his credit, Hart stayed calm when, through gritted teeth, he said, "Get your fucking security team in here now and tell them to lock this up immediately."

I looked down at the crate. Was I imagining things or had I heard a noise coming from within the metal walls? It had sounded like a soft bump but it had been so low that I wasn't sure I'd actually heard anything at all.

"All right, all right," Hines said. He went to a console on the wall that matched the one on the outer door and pressed the button. "Sam, can you get a couple of security guys to the reception room, please? And get them to find a room they can lock. One of those old offices on level 3 will be great."

"Don't you have any cells?" Hart asked.

Hines scoffed. "Why would we need cells?"

"In case you need to lock someone up."

Hines looked at him askance. "I can assure

you that we don't lock people up here. We are a peaceful community of survivors. The future of the human race, in fact. When the new world emerges from this current situation, there will be peace for the first time since mankind began."

He opened the door by which they'd entered. "Now, if you follow me, we can sort out this mess."

"The cage," Hart said.

Hines rolled his eyes. "Will be picked up shortly. You heard me call for security. Now come with me, please."

Hart turned to us. "I'll go with Hines and Ives. Stay here and make sure his security put the body somewhere safe."

"There's no need for that," Hines said from the corridor beyond the door. "My men are quite capable. Now follow me. All of you."

I looked at Hart. If I was going to take orders from anyone, it was him and not Charles Hines. Hart simply shrugged and said, "Hopefully they'll get the crate locked away quickly."

We followed Hines and Ives along a carpeted corridor that looked like it belonged in an office block rather than a secret bunker beneath a quarry and through a door into a small room that housed an oval conference table and a dozen chairs.

"Take a seat," Hines instructed, speaking as if

we were a group of accountants about to discuss a quarterly budget and not survivors of the most horrendous apocalypse to affect the human race.

"Can I get anyone anything?" he asked when we were all seated. "Coffee? Tea? Water?"

"I'd love a coffee," Doctor Ives said.

"Coming right up, Sarah." He went to a coffee machine and began to fill it.

"Mr Hines," Hart said, "We really need to discuss the matter at hand."

"Very well," Hines said once he'd got the coffee machine going. "What exactly is the matter at hand, Mr Hart? I was told by Marilyn MacDonald that you were bringing a dead body here and that Dr Ives was to be informed of its arrival as soon as it got here. Is that what's happening here or not?"

Hart shook his head. "No, it's not. There seems to be a mix up in communication somewhere."

"Well, I will admit that when I spoke to Miss MacDonald, the line was terrible. The network isn't what it used to be, you know. But I got the gist of what she was saying."

"No," Hart said, "I don't think you did."

Hines frowned. "Are you telling me that the body in that crate is not one of Sarah's dead relatives?"

Now it was Hart's turn to frown in confusion. "What?"

"A dead relative. We have them delivered here from time to time if they were in military service so they can be buried in cemetery. It gives our community members some small comfort to be able to visit the graves of loved ones. As long as the body isn't infected, we're glad to add it to our cemetery."

"You have a cemetery underground?" I asked.

Hines nodded. "Yes, it's quite lovely. Angelic music playing at all hours and dimmed lighting. Perhaps you'd like to see it before you go."

Before I could answer, Hart cut in. "Mr Hines, the body in that crate is the body of Patient Zero."

Hines, who had filled a mug with coffee and was bringing it to Dr Ives, visibly paled and dropped the mug. It shattered on the floor. "No, no, no. We don't talk about such things in this bunker, do you understand? It isn't good for the mental wellbeing of our people. We don't discuss the outside world's...problems."

Hart stood up. I could see that frustration was getting the better of him now. "Well like it or not, the outside world's problems are now inside your bunker. We were told to bring Patient Zero here and deliver it to Dr Sarah Ives." He pointed at Ives. "That is you, correct?"

She nodded meekly. “Yes, but why would you bring such a thing to me? There’s some mistake.”

“Aren’t you a scientist?”

She shook her head. “No. Well, yes, in a manner of speaking. I teach chemistry to the children here. I’m a teacher.”

“One of our best,” Hines added. “The kids love her.”

A deathly silence descended over the table as we all tried to make sense of the situation in our minds.

“Wait a minute,” I said, suddenly realising something. “You said dead relatives are brought here if they were in military service.”

Hines nodded. “That’s right.”

I turned to Ives. “And you thought that was one of your relatives being delivered?”

She nodded again. “Yes, that’s what I thought.”

“Who did you think it was? Which of your relatives is in the military?”

“My father.”

“What’s his name?”

“Locke,” she said. “Sergeant Terry Locke.”

17

"We've been sent on a wild goose chase," I told the others. "Locke didn't send us here because Dr Ives is the best person to deal with Patient Zero's body; he sent us here because he wanted to give her exclusive access to it. Probably thought she could improve her career prospects or become a hero or something. I don't know."

"My dad sent you here?" Ives asked.

"Yes," Hart said. "He made us think you would know the best thing to do with the body. Made us believe you were a scientist."

"He was always pushing me to do better," she said quietly. "When I became a teacher, he was disappointed in me. He said I could be a world famous scientist and that I was wasted in teaching. But I like working with children. I didn't want fame. And when I got married and we had our son, there was no doubt left in my mind that education was my calling. Dad was always trying to push me to do better but he never asked if that was what I wanted."

"The bloody fool!" Hart said. "He arranged to have vitally important material and documents sent to his schoolteacher daughter because he wanted her to do better? Fucking ridiculous."

"He obviously didn't know the body was slowly coming back to life," I said. "He didn't know the danger he was putting everyone in."

"It doesn't matter if he knew it or not," Hart said. "He's put countless lives in danger with his stupid bloody actions."

"Danger?" Hines asked, still pale. "Coming back to life? What's happening?"

Hart looked at him with steely eyes. "Just tell me your men have put that body somewhere secure."

"They're taking it to the disused offices on Level 2. Those doors have locks."

"What kind of locks?"

Hines shrugged. "The kind you find on an office door."

"What kind of doors?'

Hines pointed at the door of the room we were in. "The same as that one. Wooden office doors."

"Tell me about your security team."

"What about them?"

"Are they armed?"

"They have pepper spray and truncheons but I assure you they hardly ever use them. The crime rate here is—"

"We need our weapons," Hart told him.

"That's not possible. Weapons aren't allowed in the bunker. I told you, we're a peaceful community."

"You'll be a dead community if we don't get our weapons."

"They're in the bin by the outer door, waiting for you to collect them when you leave."

Hart left the room and we followed him to the waiting room. The door that led to the cement corridor was locked.

"Open this door," Hart told Hines.

Hines went to the console on the wall. "Sam, open the reception room door, please. Our guests are leaving."

"We're not leaving," Hart said. "We're getting our weapons and coming back inside."

"Not possible," Hines said as the door clicked open. "I cannot allow you to bring weapons in here. If I let you do it, then someone else will want to do it as well. Where will it end?'

"Listen closely to me," Hart said. "There's a fucking monster in your bunker. Pepper spray and truncheons aren't going to touch it."

We walked out through the door and Hines said to the man in the booth, "They're leaving, Sam."

"Very good, sir," Sam said. He pressed some buttons on his console and the next door opened, along with the door that led outside to the quarry. Obviously Bunker 53's exit protocol was nowhere near as strenuous as its entrance procedure.

"Don't close those doors, Sam," Hart told the man in the booth. "We're coming back inside in a minute.

We proceeded through the middle door, the one with the white line painted on the floor behind it and then the green line just beyond that, where our weapons were stored in the plastic bin.

Hart turned around to address Hines, who was still watching us from the waiting room.

"Don't close the doors," Hart pleaded with him. "Please."

"Good day, gentlemen," Hines said. The door behind us began to close. As it did, I saw the lights in the waiting room where Hines was standing suddenly turn red. He looked up at them, a confused look on his face. An alarm sounded, a low buzzing that repeated every two seconds.

Then an automated female voice said,

"Automatic safety lockdown will begin in ten seconds. Ten. Nine. Eight."

"Run!" Hart shouted. "We have to get out of here!"

From behind us, I could hear screams coming from within the bunker.

"Seven. Six."

We sprinted for the outer door. There was no time to collect our weapons from the plastic bin so Tanya grabbed the bin itself and dragged it along behind her.

"Five. Four."

The door behind us closed completely, cutting off the sound of the screams. I heard the locks slam into place with a metallic finality.

"Three. Two. One."

We made it through the shrinking gap in the door and out into the quarry. The outer door closed and locked.

Zero, I thought to myself.

18

We lifted off from the quarry and soared into the air. Through the visor of my flight helmet, I watched the quarry recede into the distance below us. With the camouflage netting back in place, it was impossible to tell there was anything out of the ordinary down there yet Bunker 53 was now a tomb.

With Vess running around in there, anyone who wasn't already dead soon would be.

All because an army sergeant who knew he was about to die had tried to do his daughter what he thought was a favour. His misguided familial loyalty had cost many people their lives, including the daughter he'd thought he was helping.

"You see, Lucy," Sam said through his headset. "That's what I was trying to tell you. It doesn't matter how safe you think you are, when your time is up, there's nothing you can do about it. Those people down there thought those big doors were keeping the nasty stuff out but now they're locked inside with Patient Zero. Kind of funny if you think about it."

"It isn't funny at all," Lucy said. "They only wanted to survive."

"I'm just glad the place is sealed," Hart said.

"Are we just going to leave Vess in there?" I asked him.

He shrugged against his harness. "What else can we do? The place went into automatic lockdown. We can't get in and he can't get out."

"Maybe Marilyn will have a plan," Hamilton said.

"Like what?" Hart asked him.

"I don't know. Maybe if we flooded the bunker's ventilation system with poisonous gas or something to make sure Vess is definitely dead. It would be a mercy for anyone left alive in there as well. Better to be poisoned than to get ripped apart by that monster."

"We'll see," Hart said. "Personally, if I never see that place again it'll be too soon."

We fell into a thoughtful silence and I watched the landscape below. Zombies shambled across fields and along roads. They huddled together in towns and villages. This was the world the people in Bunker 53 had tried to keep out but in the end, they'd fallen victim to it just the same as everyone else.

I wondered if there were other bunkers in different parts of the country. It would make sense that they'd be spread around and the title Bunker 53 suggested there were at least fifty-two others somewhere. If the people inside the other bunkers were as short-sighted as the people we'd just met, I didn't hold out much hope for the future of the human race.

We'd been flying for almost an hour and the landscape below had given way to sea when the pilot addressed Hart over the headsets. "Sir, we have an incoming transmission from a Brigadier James Gordon."

Hart let out a sigh that crackled in my headphones. "What the hell does he want? All right, patch him through."

Gordon's voice came through the static. "Mr Hart, I'm contacting you because you have something that was taken from me. I know you've removed it from the island. Don't ask me how I know, I just know."

"What the hell do you want, Gordon?"

"I'm asking the questions. Do you still have my item on board your chopper?"

"Why the hell should I tell you anything?"

There was a slight pause and then Gordon

said, "Have you read my notes? Well, you haven't read them of course, you're just a grunt with a gun. So let me rephrase that. Have you been told about the contents of my notes?"

Hart frowned. "Yes."

"Then you know that I have a certain device in my possession that can change people into something quite unpleasant."

"Yes, I know that," Hart said.

"I've been looking for a place to test it out. My scientists are very specific about their needs for the initial test. It has to be somewhere isolated, they said. How about a building tucked away on an island? I asked them. That will do nicely, they told me."

Hart's eyes widened. He covered his microphone with his hand and said to us, "He's planted the biological weapon at Site Brave One."

Despite the covered microphone, Gordon must have heard him because he said, "That's right, I have. Congratulations, you've figured it out. I wonder of you can figure out what will happen if you don't deliver Patient Zero's body to me."

"No, listen, we don't have it."

We were over the island now, descending to the tarmac. "Maintain present altitude," Hart told the pilot. The Chinook hovered fifteen feet from the ground. Through the open tail section, I could see the big boxy building with its silvered windows. Had Gordon really managed to plant his device in there?

"That isn't the answer I wanted to hear," Gordon said.

"You don't understand," Hart said. "It's locked away."

"You think I won't do it," Gordon said. "Very well." His voice was replaced by static.

"Gordon?" Hart asked. "Gordon, are you there?"

"The channel has gone dead, sir," the pilot said.

We all watched the Site Alpha One building. It seemed quiet enough. Maybe the Brigadier had been bluffing.

Then I realised that even if there was any noise coming from the building, we wouldn't hear it. The Chinook's rotors were too loud and the flight helmets were designed to block out any sound other than what came through the headset.

"Patch me through to Marilyn MacDonald's phone," Hart said.

"Yes, sir."

I heard a ringing in my earphones. Marilyn answered the phone immediately.

"Listen to me," Hart said. "Get everyone out of the building. Immediately."

"Sorry, Ian, I cant' hear you very well. There's something going on just outside my office."

In the background I could hear loud bangs, shouts, and screams.

"Marilyn, get out! The airborne virus is in the building!"

I heard Marilyn make a small coughing sound and then her voice rose in pitch to a blood-curdling snarl. She'd obviously dropped the phone because the next thing I heard were her footsteps walking across her office. She must have opened her office door because the noises from the corridor suddenly became louder.

Hart said, "Marilyn," one more time but it was obvious his heart wasn't in it. He knew as well as we all did what had just happened.

It was impossible to see anything through the silver reflective material on the windows but through the glass door, I could see people running. Then a gout of blood sprayed onto the glass, obscuring my vision.

"What do we do now, sir?" the pilot asked.

Hart sighed and turned his face away from the building which was now full of killing machines that had once been people. If the airborne virus worked as Brigadier Gordon's scientists hoped it would, most of the people in there would kill each other savagely.

Any survivors would be killed off by the virus in a few days.

We all looked at Hart. What could we do to help the people in the building? We all knew the answer. Just like Bunker 53, Site Bravo One was lost.

Hart took a long breath and said, "Get us out of here."

THE END

Thank you for reading the Undead Rain series. Please remember to leave a review!

To connect on Facebook, follow this link:

https://www.
facebook.com/ShaunHarbingerAuthorPage/

Printed in Great Britain
by Amazon

44955830R00097